MARTIAN DISCOVERY

It was "morning" on Mars. Now Dolph *had* to look down, come what may. He launched himself across the floor of the crate to the port-hole. He was already so used to the effects of free fall that he arrived without banging his nose more than slightly.

The view, disappointingly, was not good. The glare was blinding. But slowly, he got used to it. And slowly, he began to realize what he was seeing: the canals. Dolph drew in a sharp breath as the crate descended.

The canals of Mars were real—and before the next hour was over, he was going to become the first of all human beings to know without doubt just what they were.

Assuming, of course, that he lived through the next hour.

WELCOME TO MARS

JAMES BLISH

AVON
PUBLISHERS OF BARD, CAMELOT, DISCUS AND FLARE BOOKS

AVON BOOKS
A division of
The Hearst Corporation
959 Eighth Avenue
New York, New York 10019

Copyright © 1967 by James Blish
Published by arrangement with the Estate of James Blish
Front cover illustration by Wayne D. Barlowe
Library of Congress Catalog Card Number: 82-90805
ISBN: 0-380-63347-7

First Avon Printing, May, 1983

AVON TRADEMARK REG. U. S. PAT. OFF. AND IN
OTHER COUNTRIES, MARCA REGISTRADA, HECHO EN
U. S. A.

Printed in the U. S. A.

WFH 10   9   8   7   6   5   4   3   2   1

CONTENTS

To Dirk Sostman

FOREWORD

Mars is a badly maligned planet. Let's hope that there really are no intelligent beings on it; for if there are, they would have good cause to sue most science-fiction writers for libel.

Some time in the near future, we will know from personal experience just what Mars is like. In the meantime, we must guess, from the evidence provided by very difficult and dubious astronomical studies. The very best view that we have ever had of Mars gives us about as much information as we could gather from a photograph of an apple a city block away from the camera. (But see the Afterword, too.)

What we think we know about this small, distant planet—so much like Earth, and yet so little like it—isn't very encouraging. There are no broad, silent canals; there are no seas; there cannot be man-like creatures there, let alone creatures who flourish swords and fly airships; and the romantic twin moons are no more than sparks in the sky, and even these not visible in high latitudes. The warm spring nights of Mars are a myth—even in high summer, a man would freeze to death at sunset. The Mars of such writers as Edgar Rice Burroughs and Ray Bradbury simply does not exist.

Yet all the same, Mars is a romantic planet, instinct with mysteries much more interesting than the conventions with which fiction has invested it. It is, we may be moderately sure, a high desert unlike any wasteland we have ever seen on Earth, full of paradoxes, inexplicably marked, and teeming with its own solutions to problems which have no counterparts on Earth. And it's apparently the only other planet in the Solar System on which a brave man might just barely manage to stay alive, if he never stopped trying.

I like this semi-real Mars much better than I do the transplanted Arabia called 'Mars' in most of science fiction. In addition to being as honest a world as the few facts allow us to construct right now, it's a new theatre for a human hero. If what we find on Mars when we land there is just a well-worn stage setting, I for one will be vastly disappointed.

But I don't expect to be. In fact, if the real Mars is more than vaguely like Dolph Haertel's Mars, as he sees it in this book, even that would surprise me. However, we have tried together to look as closely as possible across the 48-million-mile gulf between us and this silent, ancient, dull-red companion world. What little we saw was beautiful.

We think you will think so, too.

JAMES BLISH

New York
1965

WELCOME TO MARS

PART ONE

On the Beach

1. THE TREE HOUSE

Dolph Haertel—even now that he was eighteen, nobody who knew him risked calling him Adolph, except his foster-father—took a quick last look at the free-floating needle in the middle of the table. Then he launched himself across the floor of his packing-crate to the port-hole, for his first close view of Mars.

The view wasn't particularly good. For one thing, the bullseye was double; he had bought it originally as raw material for a telescope mirror, and because the walls of the packing-crate were also double, he had been forced to use both blanks to make a single porthole. The result was rather like looking down at Mars through a short tunnel, six inches in diameter, with an inch-thick pane of slightly scratched crown glass at each end.

In addition, the glare was blinding. Even at only a little beyond one hundred miles above the planet's surface, Dolph was still effectively outside the Martian atmosphere, and between the sharp steel-blue glare of the gas horizon and the red-tinged lemon shimmering of the noonday desert, details were almost as washed out as they were in the best Palomar photographs.

Nevertheless, as Dolph fell slowly toward the desert
south of the area called the Sinus Sabaeus, a regular
triangle of dark blue-green streaks, narrowing from the
Sinus through the desert towards the "oasis" named
(most fancifully) Arabia, gradually took on better and
better definition. He watched them grow, hardly daring
to breathe. These dark, impossibly straight lines were
major examples of the Martian mystery long referred
to as "canals," though nothing could be more certain
than that they were not canals in any Earthly sense.
Were they volcanic fault lines? Animal trails? Something made by intelligent life, perhaps millions of years
ago? Or just illusions, put together from tiny details by
an eye straining for a regular pattern across nearly
fifty million miles of emptiness?

But these canals were not fading away as the packing-crate settled. On the contrary, they were becoming
sharper every minute. From up here—for Dolph was
now close enough to think of the diminishing gap as a
height, rather than a distance—his eye could already
resolve details smaller than fifty kilometers across, so
that he could have seen a Sicily or even a Long Island,
had Earth's areographers been whimsical enough to put
one on the map of Mars; and still the canals showed no
sign of dissolving into a welter of background markings,
as a proper optical illusion should. Instead, their lin-
earity became steadily more definite, their edges sharper
and more unarguable as he descended.

No, the canals of Mars were real—and before the
next hour was over, Dolph Haertel was going to become
the first human being in history to know without doubt
just what they were...

Outside the tree-house, spring winds moved gently in
the Iowa night. Dolph Haertel touched a bared copper
end of a wire to a B battery terminal and watched the
needle floating above the center of the breadboard rig
begin to turn slowly and uncertainly. The needle paid
as little attention to the winds outside as it did to any
other force of the massive and turning Earth. For the
needle, the breadboard was all of the universe that there
was.

At the age of seventeen, Dolph Haertal had discovered anti-gravity.

Dolph was wholly aware of the fantastic importance of what he had found, but the discovery did not seem nearly as unlikely to him as it would have to, say, his foster-father—or, for that matter, to a theoretical physicist who had spent a lifetime studying the mysterious metrical frame of space-time, that invisible, tyrannical grid which confined the courses of spiral nebulae and falling stones alike. Indeed, the discovery seemed inevitable to him now, at least in the light of hindsight.

At the very least, better than half a dozen accidents seemed to have conspired to lead him toward it—and for seeing it when he at last happened upon it, he was fully prepared to take credit if asked, for a great deal of reading in the history of science had convinced him of the truth of Pasteur's first law of research: "Chance favors only the prepared mind."

The preparation had inhered first of all in a natural bent for mathematics—part of it doubtless only that gift that exists in every child until it is suppressed or poisoned by the schools; part of it perhaps inherited from his mother, who was a government bacteriologist at N.A.S.A.'s Center of Xenobiology at the State University of Iowa in nearby Iowa City. (Certainly little of it could have descended from his foster-father, who was a grain-elevator salesman whose "head for figures"— to use Mrs. Haertel's affectionate description—"comes to a point at business arithmetic.")

Then, too, there had been the fact that his naturally rather solitary bent—even outdoors, leaning toward hikes and fishing rather than team sports like baseball, which he found acutely dull—had been furthered by a boyhood isolation imposed from outside: his foster-father spent much of his time "on the road"—which was as likely to take him to Manitoba or the Punjab as it was to any of the American bread-basket states—and as a government worker in the space sciences his mother was subject to transfers of base upon short notice, or no notice at all. Hence, although the suburban house in Iowa's low, rolling green hills was spacious and the countryside altogether pleasant, Dolph was never tempted into the mistake of thinking of it as "home"; he had never had one, and did not particularly feel the lack; and he had never been thrown among any group his own age long enough to form a firm friendship which might have drawn his attention outward from his own thoughts and the reading which chiefly nourished them.

Lately, it was true, he had taken more and more to noticing that the human beings in the world were divided into two sorts, one of which seemed softer and unarguably was more difficult to talk to than the other. One of these, a disturbing girl with black hair and blue eyes, named Nanette Ford, had even shown an astonishing comprehension of what Dolph was up to now, so much so that for a while he had hoped she might share the grand adventure itself. But more and more it had come to seem to him that the risks were too great; and besides, in a venture with so many unknowns, the including of a second party—and that a girl!— would be the least manageable of all, and the most avoidable.

The final and most crucial stroke of luck had come when he was fourteen, and already beginning to turn himself, without being aware of it, into an attic inventor—perhaps one of the last of the breed, in a world dominated by team research costing sums only governments could afford to risk or could hope to raise. (The attic itself was out, for despite his mother's intervention, Dolph's foster-father could not be swayed from the notion that all forms of experimentation involved explosions, or at least a risk of fire; but he was allowed to work in the top of the garage. Dolph carefully did not point out that when both cars were in it, the garage was almost as costly an edifice as the house; his conscience was quite clear about it, since his plans included no explosions, nor even so much as a lighted match.)

Instead, he had four years ago blundered upon a brief mathematical paper in *Nature*, that most British and yet most universal of all scientific journals, which had turned out to have a bearing on the mystery of gravity—a mystery abandoned by most physicists long ago, since the prevailing Einstein cosmography ruled firmly that nothing could be done about gravity but endure it, time without end. Since at fourteen Dolph had not yet had enough time to decide that any scientific question could be closed or any theory sacrosanct, he set out to run down all other existing papers on the subject, and to keep his eye open for new ones.

His motives for this were not entirely embedded in intellectual curiosity. Through his mother, he was closer than most laymen to the U.S. space effort, and better able to see—as he did without difficulty—what an enormously expensive blind alley it was becoming. Project Apollo, the American effort to make a manned landing on the Moon, had already consumed billions of dollars and was still utterly bogged down, its time-table advanced again and again and becoming more difficult to believe with each postponement. Even simple unmanned rocket shots did not seem to be gaining much in reliability, though they certainly never failed to be more costly than their predecessors. Wasn't there some more sensible way to go about the whole thing?

Apparently not; and yet, the spectacle offended Dolph. He was wholly susceptible to the vast romance inherent—though not yet realized—in space travel, and it seemed to him that the way the world was going about prosecuting it was crazy; or, at least, that the people in charge had lost sight of the primary goal, which was to get out into space. Instead, the whole world seemed to be spending itself blind on more and more expensive rockets—not because these brute-force engineers' toys were the best way to cross interplanetary space (that question apparently hadn't even been raised), but because it was a useful substitute for the arms race that had kept the now-obsolete Cold War going. Apparently taxpapers could still be sold spaceships—even dud ones—where they could no longer be sold missiles.

All right; Dolph knew he wasn't competent to question the politics of it, nor indeed was he much interested in that side of it. He was interested in space travel itself, and he was too young to be convinced that rockets were the only possible devices that could free man of the Earth. It occurred to him that if gravity was the chief enemy of spaceflight, then something might be gained by studying the enemy, no matter how hopeless Relativity declared such a study would turn out to be.

The outcome was that at seventeen Dolph had become an amateur expert in a field so new that few physicists even knew it existed, and most would say it could not exist. For all its formidable reputation, Relativity had turned out to be absurdly easy to master— a discovery which has been made over and over again by everyone with any feeling for the poetry of maths— and full of absurdly large holes in both its reasoning and its appeals to evidence. British scientists in particular, it turned out, had been shooting holes in poor old Einstein for more than a decade, and one especially drastic English astonomer, a mystical don named Milne, had produced a competing form of Relativity that swallowed Einstein's like a gnat. Milne had died nearly twenty years before Dolph's birth, but he was not forgotten—not in a suburb of Iowa City, anyway.

Dolph doodled with Milne, and Dingle, and the pitifully few others who had had the courage to keep on thinking about gravity; and having been born into precisely the right moment, and having brought precisely the right mind to the right opportunity, fell into the fundamental discovery that although gravity is (as Einstein had maintained) a condition of space rather than a force like electricity, it has polarity (which Einstein had broken his heart trying to disprove). It followed naturally that it could be manipulated, probably without too much work; since it was a weak field to begin with, and worked best only over very long distances, only a little effort should be required to produce desirable vector effects—

Or, that is, working *with* gravity rather than against it could probably be done in a garage, with only a few dollars. For example: a model space drive, capable of lifting perhaps a hundred pounds or more of dead weight, should be easy to assemble from standard television set parts, and other cheap, available components.

With Nanette's rather distracting help, he had assembled a small breadboard rig to test at least a few small margins of the notion. The rig worked only too well. It turned out to be well over a hundred times as efficient as he had dared to hope. In an eternal moment of groaning boards and squeaking nails, it had cut the whole garage off from the Earth and lifted it, both family cars included, a good inch off its foundations. The instant when the power cut off and the whole mass thudded back into place was even more alarming, but it was all that had saved garage, Nanette and Dolph; he had had the rig plugged into a light socket, and the feeder line had parted before the frame building had pulled quite free of its concrete bedding.

Nanette had been frightened, without knowing precisely what had happened or why, but it hadn't occurred to Dolph to be genuinely alarmed until a day later, when some of the implications of the test began to pile up in his imagination. After all, despite his miscalculation there had never been any real danger that the garage would take off for the clouds. It was too massive a load for the available power; hoisting it and its contents far enough to snap a BX cable was quite incredible enough, without imagining consequences the breadboard rig could never have brought about.

But there were things the breadboard rig could do. One of them, he realized, was to make possible a small but genuine spaceship—so small that he could build it himself, in the back yard, but fully functional all the same.

When the idea came to the surface, he *was* scared.

And yet—why not? Obviously the first manned space journey, even to so nearby a target as the Moon, was still decades in the future for the money-happy engineers, their brute-force rockets, and their professionally heroic "astronauts." Dolph could see no good reason— no good technical reason, anyhow—why the breadboard rig should not take him to Mars some time within a year, provided that he could somehow scrounge about two hundred dollars... well, call it three hundred to be on the safe side... and could find the time both to do the building job properly, and to make the round trip before somebody caught him at it and forbade his trying it at all.

It was primarily out of the need for disguise that the tree-house had evolved, much to the satisfaction of Mr.

Haertel, who though he used the outdoors for nothing
more strenuous than business golf himself, liked to see
his adopted son get his nose out of books and tackle
something, anything that was properly boyish and out-
doorsy. The ancient pear tree in the back yard would
have been absurdly easy for anyone to climb, except
possibly for somebody who had to try it in a wheelchair;
but the very fact that the tree-house was up off the
ground made it unlikely to be blundered into by adults
who might find what was inside it unexpected enough
to prompt questions. As for kids, well, there was nobody
around Dolph's own age who would think a tree-house
anything but too juvenile to be worth noticing, except
Nanette; and younger children could invade it whenever they liked, as far as Dolph was concerned—there
would be nothing in it complex enough for them to
damage, and nothing for them to see that they could
report to older people in any terms which would make
sense.

He made a model ship of his first packing-case, in
the ravine with which the parcel of land ended at the
back. He caulked it as carefully as though it would some
day actually need to hold breathable air against the
malice of a hard vacuum—though his limited resources
prevented his giving it a double hull or any insulation—and equipped it with his first breadboard rig.
One night, far past midnight, he lifted it silently a
hundred feet into the moonlit air, and just as silently
set it down again except for a faint grating noise as its
bottom resettled among the heather-hazed rocks of the
dry stream bed. Nobody saw the boxy spectre as far as
he could tell—although the neighbor's dog, a pure-bred
cocker spaniel with nerves of purest Jello, howled all
the rest of the night—and a week later he felt sure
enough of the safety of the model to take Nanette along
for a second cautious night ascension. She was breath-
less with excitement, but he took great care to make
the "flight" as slow and solemn as that of a tethered
balloon, and to avoid even the faintest hint that there
might be more to be done with the anti-gravity field
than this. (And he swore her to secrecy on even that
much of it.)

The tree-house was not much larger than the model, but it was altogether more elaborate. He meant it to take him into space, and to bring him back; he had no intention that it should kill him instead, if he could possibly avoid that. The floor of the exterior crate went into the tree first, as a platform (which, like the sides, had been sprayed with five layers of epoxy resins over the basic caulking—a horribly expensive procedure because he had been forced to buy the spray in household-size aerosol cans from the local supermarket, for the sake of secrecy). A sixth outside layer he had had to mix himself; it consisted of high-purity zinc oxide in a silicone resin base, which, an article in *Science* had reported, would strongly reflect light in the wave-lengths between 0.20 and 0.80 microns, where about 66 per cent of the Sun's output was concentrated. Then the interior crate, similarly caulked, had been bedded on the platform in a nest of rock wool, the best he could do in the way of insulation (it would at least preserve some heat balance in space, though against hard radiation it would be worse than useless), and set about preparing his entrance lock and his porthole.

The problems of supply had to be ducked, for the most part. He could not afford to buy, and he would not have the space to carry, more than a token ration of food, water or oxygen—especially oxygen, which came in expensively heavy steel bottles which had to be cracked by expensively heavy apparatus: instead, he bought his oxygen by the 22-liter flask from the local drug store, in the form of a gaseous patent medicine put on the market for hypochondriacs who were nervous about smog. Again, this was a sinfully expensive way of attacking the problem at hand, but no other was open to Dolph if disguise was to be maintained.

There was no solution to this logistic problem, nor to the menace of cosmic rays and the solar wind, but that of time. The dinosaurs of power and money might afford to tackle them directly—though they'd been doing badly at it up to now—but for Dolph only speed, eva-siveness, foreplanning and penury could serve. These were precisely what the anti-gravity drive made pos-

sible, otherwise the whole notion of the trip would be
no more than a nocturnal fantasy.

The new rig was no longer, strictly speaking, a
breadboard-chassis improvisation, though it was spaced
out almost as much for ease of access. The components,
all transistorized except for a 6BQ5 power tube, were
now fixed on a heavy table, which in turn was firmly
bolted to both the floor and one wall of the crate, and
under which was slung a set of nickle-cadmium batteries bought as surplus. The small, heavy torus which
was the source of the field was mounted on a post precisely at the crate's geometrical center, on gymbals from
a Navy-surplus gyroscopic compass.

The supplies were in; the tree-house was tight; the
rig was working; his course was plotted. There was no
longer any reason to hang back. Even his time was
accounted for, closely enough so that in a little while
it would start running out. There was a four-day week-
end coming up, and through the medium of his shop-
ping—which had been too extensive to be hidden,
though it could be disguised—Dolph had let it be known
that he planned another solitary camping trip, which
would run at least one more day than the official hol-
iday. Since he had accumulated the extra day off from
school and his marks were mostly up to snuff, the plan
aroused no unusual attention.

Of course Nanette would suspect something like the
truth when she saw the tree-house gone, but he counted
on her to keep her own counsel about it. As for the
adults, what they would think of that couldn't be helped,
but he was pretty sure their guesses would be wide of
the mark. It would probably take them two days to look
up far enough to notice that the packing-case was miss-
ing—a tree without a crate in its branches being so
much more ordinary a sight than a tree with one—and
probably they would then assume that he'd disassem-
bled it and set it up at a distance.

His foster-father, in fact, was almost sure to say:
"After all, it couldn't very well have flown away by
itself, could it?"

So that was that. Late that Thursday night, with no
more than a minimum shower of pear leaves and a yap

of stifled terror from the distant cocker, he edged the crate out of the ancient tree.

And promptly at 2207 Sidereal Time, as the calculations required, the packing-crate silently became a spaceship and vanished, Dolph and all.

2. THE SEA OF STREAMS

No amount of reading of the synthetically excited copy about orbital flights poured out by the popular press—most of it written by reporters who had been mocking the very notion of spaceflight as "that crazy Buck Rogers stuff" even after the launching of Sputnik I—had prepared Dolph for the immense fullness of space.

He had expected it to be lonely. Even the most cursory knowledge of the distance which stretched around the planets would have forewarned him that the universe of night is vast beyond all hope of understanding. When the idea of making a crossing to Mars had first come to him, one of his first thoughts had been the sober realization that Columbus in his fragile bark had been setting out to jump a local puddle compared to the audacity of setting sail for Mars in a packing-crate. The Earth itself was only barely large enough a vessel to risk in space, as the eternal lifelessness of the Moon preached graphically. The stars were suns, but their planets only motes in their eternal light.

But that space itself should truly be a sea, unappeasably in motion everywhere and charged to bursting

with restless particles and energies in every millimeter
of its measureless reaches, was a concept he had never
encountered (though he might have been warned by
the physicists' word for the phenomenal universe,
"plenum," which means, "the fullness"). The impact of
the experience itself, piled atop the shock of actually
seeing the Earth become just another point of light, lost
amid millions of others—for since Dolph was traveling
in the Galactic plane, and the position of Mars at the
time was on the other side of the Earth from Shapley
Center, the heart of the Galaxy, the Earth for him was
quickly swamped out in the general glitter of the Milky
Way—was a complete shock, and a blackly frightening
one.

In his first hour beyond the atmosphere, after he had
finished his first check-out of his crate and his course,
he became grimly aware that if he were to turn back
now he might just barely have the great good luck to
get home alive—and never mind the catastrophic nonsense of even dreaming of reaching Mars. Nothing but
luck could explain his having stayed alive this long.
Outside the packing-crate, mostly invisible and beyond
the detection of his few toy instruments, the currents
of space raged in a storm that had been going on for
fourteen billion years—if indeed it had ever had a beginning—and might go on raging for another fourteen
billion, or forever. Sun- and starlight glared off the
silicone-painted hull of his absurd shell, charring the
wood underneath steadily and implacably, molecule by
molecule. The solar wind—that torrent of atomic fragments which extended the Sun's atmosphere out as far
as Jupiter—seethed and roiled in the magnetic field
which was secondary to his miniature gravitational
pattern. X-rays from the hearts of exploding stars poured
through the ship, and its pilot too. Cosmic rays—the
stripped cores of atoms, driven at near-light velocities
from the ultimate synchrotrons of spiral galaxies—bul-
leted past him, most of them luckily deflected by his
field, missiles against which any physical shield would
have been useless. Micro-meteors, some few as big as
grains of sand, scored the paint and pitted the porthole;
these too were slowed and veered away by his field, and

those few that got through his outer hull were trapped by his insulation (although nothing could be done about the minute slow leaks these produced).

He had known about most of these things in advance, at least in the abstract, and had tried to take them into account. He had chosen for the flight a period of clear solar weather, in a trough of the pulsation cycle when no flares were expected (though there were no guarantees against them, either). Against other radiation he counted mainly on the protection of speed, to keep his dosages down to safe levels, since shielding was out of the question. With meteors he was willing to take his chances—they were not very common beyond Earth's immediate gravitational envelope, and one capable of killing him—one, say, as big as a fleck of gravel—would find him a small and gravitationally unattractive target. As for the air, the drug-store oxygen bottles were equipped with their own masks which he could don if the oxygen tension became dangerously low—though for loss of pressure in the cabin, there was again no effective precaution but speed of transit.

It had all seemed at least possible, if not very reasonable, back in the safety of the garage and the Iowa spring. In the raging sea of streams which was the reality of "empty" space, it was death, not pear-leaves, that whispered every second just outside the packing-crate.

But he was not going to turn back now—and most especially if he might not make it home alive even if he did. He had firm objections to being killed, but above all he was not going to let himself be knocked out of the sky for a project he'd already given up. All right, he'd obviously made a mistake, and a fat one—quite big enough to kill him. But he'd made it, and he was on his way. And that was that.

He tried to keep his mind off the universe of whispering blind hostility just outside by concentrating on the mechanics of his journey, but there was really very little to do. His flight plan had been the ultimate in simplicity, thanks to the fundamental nature of the discovery which had made it possible at all: the discovery that gravity is not only a structural condition

in space, as Einstein had postulated, but at the same
time a part of the general field which included electricity and magnetism as its other aspects (as Einstein
had never succeeded in proving) and hence has polarity—can have its own peculiar forms of negative and
positive poles.

Knowing only this much—and given the slight vector thrust to turn it to account—Dolph could sling himself and his tree-house away from the Earth with all
the initial velocity he could glean from Earth's own
centrifugal force, simply by shielding himself from his
planet's gravity; he had only to be careful how suddenly
he did it. Once free of the last clinging wisps of Earth's
air, he could add an acceleration of two gravities—
another sixty-four feet per second, every second—with
the snap of a switch which would in effect give the
packing-crate a "like charge" to that of the Earth: this
on top of a velocity imparted by coming off the end of
a four-thousand-mile-long sling which all his life had
been whirling him through space at the rate of not
much under a thousand miles an hour (and had he
started from the equator, it would have been greater
still).

Two gravities would not have seemed like much of
an acceleration to the rocket masters at Cape Kennedy,
who were accustomed to sweat blood (and money) to
crack their vehicles up past nine; but two gravities applied over several hours can build up a much more
respectable end-velocity than can nine gravities
achieved in the three or four minutes before a rocket
blurts out the last of its reaction-mass and becomes just
another one of the universe's helplessly falling or coast-
ing objects. And for Dolph, this much was for free, or
so near to it as made no difference. If he wanted to add
more to it, he could reject the Sun's gravity as well, at
no extra cost but some much more complicated calculations; but for a crossing as short as the one he planned,
the gain did not prove to be worth the extra brainwork.

Steering, of course, was not so easy, but here again,
a little vectoring returned large dividends. Once the
Earth's field was screened out and the crate rode free
in the sea of streams, retreating from the Sun, a faint

softening of the lines of force on the side of the crate toward Mars let in a faint tendril of the red planet's own distant tug—not much, only a sort of an urge, but enough to start him into a long curving fall towards the fleeing world. For him, after all, there was no place else to fall to.

The moment the meters first registered that tug, Dolph was able to step it up; double it, in fact. By the middle of his second day in space he was already slightly more than half-way there, and beginning to stop the Martian attraction back down and use the Earth as a drag-anchor.

It was just as well, too. The air in the crate was already thin and a little foul, and Dolph was beginning to feel quite chilly. In addition, he felt a little feverish, which he hoped was due solely to the fact that he had had no sleep, and that he hadn't been able to provide his crude vessel with plumbing. If the odd feverishness also meant that he had got a higher radiation dose than he had planned on, there wasn't a thing he could do about it. He was lucky—though he tried hard not to think about it—to be still alive at all.

But now his stern chase of Mars was beginning to show fruits. The red spark was getting fatter—not larger, exactly, but markedly brighter. From here on out the ballistics of the trip would be even simpler; he had only to fall, as mindlessly as Newton's apple, and let natural law do the rest until it was time to slow himself down to leaf-fall speed.

Not that it would do to allow carelessness or neglect to cancel out everything the sea of streams had been unable to sweep away from him. He had to land safely on Mars; he had to live there, for an hour or so at the least; and he had to get back, with proofs. Otherwise he had risked not only his own life for nothing, but also all the love and care that had brought him into the world, and kept him alive and happy until that moment a few months ago when he had decided to leave it for a while. Even here he was not really alone.

He had brought with him years of devotion, centuries of history, ages of evolution; and out here, he stood for them all, he and his scraps of Earth wood and paint and metal, of life and curiosity and knowledge. He was custodian of all these things, not just his own life.

Stub of pencil in hand, he studied his instruments with minute care, and scribbled calculations on the wall of the crate. Mars got fatter. The crate got colder.

By "morning"—though he still had been unable to sleep—the air was very bad, and he had to don the oxygen mask, after a last gulp of his K rations and swallow of water. The gas made him feel more alert, and a little warmed, too, though he knew that that part of it was an illusion. Inside the crate the light was now quite orange, cast in a truncated cone through the port-hole from the surface of Mars.

Now he *had* to look down, come what may. He took a last quick measurement from the free-floating needle in the middle of his instrument table, and then launched himself across the floor of the crate to the porthole. He was already so used to the effects of free fall that he arrived without banging his nose more than slightly.

The view, disappointingly, was not good. For one thing, the micro-meteorite scratches on the outside bull's-eye had got worse; and the glare was blinding, especially after so many hours of star-hazed blackness. But slowly, he got used to it.

And slowly, he began to realize what it was that he was seeing: the canals. They were not dissolving, but becoming steadily more definite as he descended. He drew in a sharp breath.

The canals of Mars were real—and before the next hour was over, he was going to become the first of all human beings to know without doubt just what they were.

Always providing, of course, that he lived through the next hour.

3. DOWN ... AND OUT

The oasis toward which he was settling, in the heart
of the sub-desert called Aeria, was shown on his Pic du
Midi map but not given any name—probably because
it was one of those Martian features which failed to
show up from time to time, as even larger green areas
failed to do some summers. It was an oval blotch about
thirty degrees south of the equator, and perhaps five
hundred miles off the eastern "shore" of Syrtis Major.

It was certainly showing nicely this summer. At a
guess, Dolph would have said it was as big as Rhode
Island. Five canals converged on it, and more were becoming visible, like railroad lines converging on a city,
animal trails leading to a water-hole—or spall-marks
around a bullet-hole in shatterproof glass.

Dolph resisted that last comparison until it was impossible to fight it any longer ... until, in fact, he could
see that it was very close to the truth. The nameless
oasis was an impact crater, like Meteor Crater in Ar-
izona, or the ringwalls of the Moon.

The discovery made his heart sink, for it instantly
made disastrous sense of the surface of Mars, map and

landscape both. Was it possible that Mars, too, was a
bombarded and blasted planet, as implacably lifeless
and hostile as the Moon despite its blanket of thin air?
True, it was not as obviously pocked and torn up as the
lunar landscape, but that might only mean that the
winds—and the gigantic sandstorms that they carried,
often big enough to be seen all the way from Earth—
had worn down the oldest and the biggest craters and
mountain ranges, and smoothed off the others. The retreat of the North polar snows in the spring had revealed one mountain range, the Mountains of Mitchell;
and recurrent sharp edges to the cloud-patterns had
hinted at similar ranges elsewhere on the planet, even
though no shadows of such peaks had been seen.

The roughly circular shapes of the northern de-
serts—Electris, Eridania, Ausinia, Hellas, Argyre—
also looked much like the circular maria of the Moon,
as did such smaller southern ones as Isidis Regio. And
here in the packing-crate, from less than fifteen miles
up, there was no longer any doubt that Mars at some
time in its history had been the target of vast celestial
missiles, some of them as big as asteroids. The major
canals, the ones even old Schiaparelli had seen, were
colossal straight faults in the very crust of the planet,
where whole continental blocks of the surface had tilted
like ice-floes and refrozen out of true to the main mass.
The minor canals—the radiating marks—were spalled
cracks centered upon the impacts of smaller meteors,
objects of the size that had so devastated the Moon.

Since the surface of Mars had not changed permanently since the invention of the telescope, it seemed
likely that no such cataclysm had hit Mars in more
than three hundred years. But the same thing might
be said of the Moon—which did not make Earth's sister
world any less barren and hopeless. Whenever the bombardment had struck Mars, it had changed the planet
decisively. In the sand sample that the first unmanned
Martian probe had photographed, back in 1972, there
had been many microscopic shells, like those of Earthly
Foraminifera, which showed decisively that Mars had
once had seas. They were all gone now, and the sands
of their bottoms blew about the planet in the thin gales.

Most of that water must have poured into the fissures opened when the great meteors struck, and boiled away, to go finally into combination with the rock in the form of limonite, the hydrated iron oxide which in powdered form made up the bulk of the Martian sands. Little enough was left to form the thin polar icecaps.

Had there been any highly organized forms of life on Mars back then, they could hardly have survived the sudden remaking of their whole world. If life itself had survived at all, it must have had to begin all over again. Any that survived there now, on this very ancient little world, must—paradoxically—be very primitive, and even genetically almost without memory of the age of oceans.

Mars was still not dead. But what life remained must be staging a last stand, quite as dramatically as Lowell had guessed...but with far fewer resources, and with even less hope.

Glumly, Dolph maneuvered his clumsy craft down toward a landing in the middle of the nameless oasis, the blue-green spot of life created by the stony monster from space that had also helped to turn most of Mars into a permanent desert. He had not expected anything better, really, but he had had hopes. Now, his hopes were limited to seeing just how high a form of primitive life could manage to hang on where properly there should be no life at all.

The tilted ocher tableland spread out beneath him, and the rim of the crater expanded like an opening mouth. From a mile above the desert surface he was able to see the shadows cast by the low rim, and the inside of the oasis began to look first like a bowl, and then more like a shallow saucer.

It was mid-afternoon on the desert when the packing-crate reached it, and the low domed peaks of the rim—so oddly like the hills of eastern Iowa except for their color—rose around him. As the floor of the crater came to meet him, however, he found himself in a sort of gentle blue-green twilight; the rays of the brilliant but shrunken sun did not reach to the bottom at this hour.

At last the scene outside the porthole became mo-

tionless. Cautiously, Dolph cut off his field. The crate
dropped the last few feet with a soft, muffled *thunk*, as
though it had fallen on to a mattress. Then there was
silence.

He was on Mars.

The silence continued, indifferent and undisturbed.
He had been used to it in space, because he had expected
it; but here, it was as though the planet, bent upon
cherishing the last of its own life, did not even notice
his existence. Well, why should it? In its long, slow,
tortured life, Dolph was only the accident of an instant.

He shook off his depression and set to work. First,
the outside temperature, and the air pressure.

The resulting readings were hard to believe. He took
two more of each, and could hardly trust them even
after they agreed with the first. After all, his equipment
was far from the best.

But it was the best he had, and it said that the temperature out there was twenty-five degrees Centigrade,
or 77° on the obsolete Fahrenheit scale the English-
speaking people clung to. That was outright balmy—
nobody could fairly call it less. As for the air pressure—
200 millibars—it was about equivalent to what he would
have encountered high in the Himalayas, far from
breathable even had it contained enough oxygen; but
even so it was better than twice the pressure he could
even have hoped to find up on the desert. On Mars, it
appeared, it paid to be at the bottom of a deep, deep
hole.

In short, he could go outside, wearing no more clothing than he had on right now, and with no more protection from the air than the respirator and goggles.
He put them on, followed by the canvas belt which held
the twenty plastic vials which were for his samples,
and loaded his pockets. Then he dropped to his hands
and knees before the tightly caulked barrel which was
his airlock.

A few moments later he was out. He lost about twenty
per cent of the Earthly air in the crate in the process,
but this did not bother him; he was not, after all, plan-
ning to stay long. He got to his feet and looked about.

In the indirect sunlight, the vast circular valley was

so still that it was like being on the floor of some long-untended aquarium or pond. Overhead, the sky was a deep violet, almost an indigo, in which he could see a scattering of stars, including several brilliant ones. He wondered if one of those could be the Earth. The idea gave him a distinct chill.

The horizon was near, but not bounded by the mountains of the ringwall—in fact, he could not even see their peaks on the far side; the oasis was too big for that. Except for low, rolling hills, the crater floor stretched away evenly in all directions, an almost uniform blue-green, with a few chocolate spots.

He struck a wooden match against the crate. Nothing happened, of course.

The blue-green was vegetation; he got back down on his hands and knees to look at it, then snatched his hands up again. The air was warm, all right, but the ground was bitter cold even through his gloves. He had forgotten that the midnight temperatures here probably hit 150 degrees below zero Fahrenheit during most of the year, and could not be much warmer even in high summer. Luckily his hiking shoes were heavy, and so were his socks, or he'd be risking frost-bitten toes just standing here.

The vegetation was curious stuff; he found it hard to think of anything to compare it with. In texture it was a little like loosely woven sponge, the filaments either grey, greenish or the chocolate-brown he had noticed, and looking rather tough. Interwoven with these were more delicate filaments of lighter, more vivid green, which here and there was gathered into small knots or clumps within the holes formed by the spongy matrix.

He pulled at it experimentally. It tore readily, a little to his surprise, and the fragment of it in his hand promptly seemed to shrink, forming itself into a rough ball. Similar balls, of varying sizes, were scattered about him, as though detached by a wind.

Close up, the sponge had a speckled appearance, because both kinds of filaments bore tiny fruits or bladders, he could not decide which. Those on the tough filament were black or brown like their parents and

were about the size of B-B shot; those on the green
strands were bigger and elongated, like small beans,
but were quite transparent. Suspecting water or some
sap, Dolph stripped off a glove and tried to break one
of these sacs with the thumb and finger nail, but its
pellicle, though it yielded, would not break.

Water on second thought was unlikely, since it would
freeze in the Martian night. But what then was in the
clear little bladders?

He was distracted from the question by a sign of
movement on his bare palm. Startled, he looked closer.
The skin seemed to be crawling.

It *was* crawling. He was reminded at once of what
had happened in his boyhood when he had picked up a
wounded robin chick, and had afterwards discovered
that his hand was covered with mites, an incident which
had divested him of all sentimentality toward birds
forever. These were not mites, but they were some Martian equivalent. They were about a quarter of an inch
long, looked quite like some species of nematode or
roundworm, and there were thousands of them. And
yes, here and there among them were genuinely mite-
like creatures, black arthropods scuttling among the
nematodes, or settled quietly on the backs of their necks,
feeding...

He kicked away the sponge around him in a hurry
until he had exposed a patch of powdery red soil, and
scrubbed both hands in a handful of it, cold or no cold.
Though he probably had no reason to be afraid of these
tiny spots of Martian animal life, he was not going to
take any of it back into the crate with him—and hence
back to Earth—if he could possibly help it. At least not
loose on his person or in his clothing.

But he did want samples. The vegetation alone was
a discovery worth the trip. The 1978 unmanned probe
had brought back no life but a few unexciting species
of bacteria, and some spore-like things which had refused to germinate on Earth. This spongy stuff was
evidently a kind of lichen—half-fungus, half-alga—
highly developed to wring from the inhospitable soil,
air and sunlight what little nutriment and energy they
offered. Its tendency to break into balls when it reached

a critical size, furthermore, meant that up on the surface it must travel with the winds when the summer air circulation set in—thus explaining the mysterious "wave of darkening" which swept down from the polar icecap when it melted, and explained as well why the dark maria could never be permanently covered by the sandstorms. It was a lichen, but it had adopted the spawning habit of the tumbleweed.

Where did it get water? Surely there wasn't enough water vapor in the air to be worth bothering with—certainly not enough to support the acres and acres of life about him, and by extension, over all the dark areas of the planet. After a moment's puzzlement the answer came to him; the fungal strands probably broke it chemically out of the sand, for every molecule of limonite carries with it, in chemical combination, three molecules of water. That way, the plant could get its water need without even touching or needing a drop of water in the liquid state. At high noon, some of those water molecules would break free at the urging of sunlight and scurry for new strategic positions, carrying other essential chemicals with them by loose bonding rather than in any sort of conventional solution. Some Earthly desert plants, the xerophytes, had the rudiments of a similar system for using bound water; it was what occasionally made specimen cactuses in museum cases suddenly sprout after decades of apparent lifelessness—and what kept alive grains of wheat which, buried thousands of years ago with the Pharaohs, sometimes astonished biologists by germinating. Here on Mars it was not an oddity, however, but a basic mechanism of life.

Feeling a little dazed, Dolph carefully stuffed fragments of the sponge into four of his vials, scrubbing his hands again afterwards—and the outsides of the vials, too. If his guess was correct, at least some of the material would be alive when he got home.

After a last look at the sky he went back inside the crate, where he transferred samples from one of the vials on to several pre-poured agar plates. He doubted that they would take hold, but there was no harm in trying. With his oxygen mask off he found the task, light though it was, a little tiring. A check with the barometer showed that his cabin pressure was down to an Earthly equivalent of eight thousand feet—doubtless due to losses through the airlock. Well, if Andean Indians could live and do heavy labor at that altitude, so could he, at least for a while.

And now what? It might be worthwhile lifting ship and taking a look at some other spot. On the other hand, there was no reason to suppose that any other vegetated area would differ significantly from this one, despite its isolation. Searching for possible ruins, like mapping or any other form of protracted exploration, was out of the question—it was beyond his equipment and his available time. After all, this trip was essentially only a stunt, and it would be sensible not to forget it.

All the same, he could see no special reason why he should not levitate a mile or so above the desert—which would certainly put him above any possible mountains—and let the planet turn under him for a while, just to make a quick survey in the hope of seeing something interesting. If he stayed aloft only a few hours he could traverse as much as a sixth of the planet westward, crossing Syrtis Major and probably Isidis Regio too, and perhaps reaching the eastern marches of Aethiopis, where there was a chain of oases all far bigger than this one.

Well, after all, why not? He could spare four hours before he had to leave for home; that would even leave him a margin for error. He secured everything—quickly, though, because the afternoon was fading and he wanted to drift west in the remaining sunlight, trusting to the long shadows to betray anything really striking on the surface. Then he fed power into the rig.

Nothing happened.

Alarmed, he checked the leads, but everything was tight. The coil was intact, too, and shorting the battery produced a nice, fat spark-shower.

Yet the crate simply refused to lift.

Baffled, Dolph set about running a component-by-component check, grimly doing his best to keep his breathing even and shallow and his hands steady. The shadowless semi-dusk outside was becoming slowly but steadily dimmer, and above all he did not want to be caught on Mars overnight.

It did not, in fact, take him very long to find the trouble. It was in the one logically vulnerable spot in the system, and the one about which he could do precisely nothing: the 6BQ5 power tube. It was burned out.

Of course, he should have brought a spare; he realized that now. It wouldn't have taken up much space. But he hadn't.

Almost any other failure in the rig, Dolph could have repaired—it was otherwise not much more complicated than a crystal radio—but this one was fatal. The tube had been brand new, and had tested out perfectly the day before he'd left Earth, but that was no comfort now. Once a tube goes, it is gone, regardless of age. This one was dead.

And Dolph was marooned.

4. A LITTLE DETECTION

Though it was small consolation to Dolph, he could reflect—and it looked like he might have plenty of time for that—that part of his trouble was rooted in the early discovery of the transistor, found before the vacuum tube—or "thermionic valve"—had had a chance to come of age. Even in its heyday, now a decade gone, tube design had been more of an art than a science, depending almost as much upon a feeling for shapes and flows as on calculations of the mean free paths of electrons. As a result, a well-designed tube might function perfectly in any of a hundred uses for thousands of hours— or it might fail an hour after passing its final tests at the factory, and not even its designer could tell the successes from the lemons. Dolph's solitary and crucial 6BQ5 had evidently been a lemon.

But the real failure, he knew very well, had been in his own foresight.

Yet there was no time to be wasted in self-reproaches or in idle detective work. Dusk was falling fast, and the temperature even faster; at this rate it would be freezing outside by sunset. Yet, too, there would be no point

43

in lurching about inside the packing-case in a panic. He could not afford the loss of a drop of water, a cubic centimeter of oxygen or an erg of energy in waste motion. He needed first of all to run an inventory of what he had—and then to think about how he might best use it.

And it had to be a detailed inventory—right down to the last thread. He could depend upon Mars for nothing, this early; he could not even hope.

Oxygen first. He had started with five flasks, totaling 110 liters or 45 gallons at Earth-normal pressure, stored at 300 pounds per square inch. One flask was probably almost gone, and the drug-store gadget had no gauge to tell him how much was left. Undoubtedly his total store would last him the night, but he had to hope for much more time than that. He scribbled furiously on the walls of the crate.

Ideally, he might seal the crate well enough to keep the air pressure inside it at about one half of one Earth atmosphere, using Mars's own nitrogen to pressurize the room if he could rig a way to pump it in enough of a hurry. But if he did that, he would need an oxygen volume of 40 per cent—twice Earth's—in order to keep up the necessary oxygen pressure of 160 mm. of mercury, and his supplies simply wouldn't permit it, even over a short-term. On the other hand, if he tried to maintain full Earth air pressure in the crate, he would need a lot of power, and that was in short supply too—no more than remained in his batteries.

No immediate solution was obvious. All right, shelve it for now.

Water: possibly not a real worry yet. He had three 17.5 gallon drums of it—storage drums from the Civil Defense craze of 1962. The drums were each 22 ¼ inches high and stacked one on another in one corner of the crate, leaving him four inches of headroom for unstacking them. Each had a plastic bag liner assembly with a spout which folded under its cover; one could be used as a commode by cutting the mouth of the liner and folding it around the top opening of the drum. When about seven-eighths full, the liner could be sealed with a wire tie—and saved, he thought with grimness that

left him no room to be squeamish, for fertilizer or half
a dozen other easily imaginable uses, plus others that
would doubtless occur to him if he lived long enough.

He was not foolish enough to believe that 52.5 gallons could be called a lot of water. In the dessicated air
of Mars he would have to consume a minimum of a
gallon a day, not counting probably that much again
lost by evaporation—probably being lost right now,
right through the plastic liners. But there was life on
Mars, and that meant there was water too. He thought
that he might find enough to use in the three weeks to
a month that the contents of the drums should give
him.

Now, food. He had a small case of K rations, what
the specifications advertised as a two weeks' supply,
which meant that it could be stretched to last as long
as the water in the drums would. Thereafter, he would
again have to see what he could find on Mars—and
face the excellent chance that all the life here would
prove poisonous to him. He also had a small packet of
agar-agar and a jar of Bovril which he had brought
along as food for cultures of Martian micro-organisms,
but he was sure he would have no objections to beef
aspic for himself instead—again, for so long as there
was water to make it with. That might keep him alive
another week. What else? Oh, yes: six cans of evaporated milk, and two ounces of salt. And...one month's
supply of multi-vitamin capsules, if he stretched it to
the utmost. Where might he get more? That any life-
form on Mars might contain any vitamin that he needed,
let alone all of them, was close to impossible.

All right, shelve that too. He had to hope.

Power? The nickel-cadmium batteries, indefinitely
rechargeable. Surely something could be done about
that. Something had to be done, for he would need power
to keep up the air pressure, and probably also to generate oxygen by electrolysis of water if he could find
water, and certainly to generate heat if he could think
of no way to store heat during the day. The only other
stored power he had with him was a small can of Sterno,
which he did not dare even think of lighting until his
oxygen problem could be made less acute. Nothing else

was available but muscle power, which would not last
long if Mars could not be made to refuel it.

His clothing, counting what he had on, consisted of
three pairs of long, heavy wool socks; two T-shirts; two
pairs of boxer shorts and one of athletic shorts; two
flannel shirts; one pair of heavy slacks; a pair of hiker's
shoes; a pair of heavy gloves; a racing driver's helmet
liner and a pair of heavy, padded, tinted goggles; a thick
jacket, and a voluminous wool muffler. Not bad in terms
of the warmth needed, but he had to remember that all
of it would wear rapidly on this harsh world—and rot
rapidly, too, because he would be unable to wash any
of it, let alone himself.

But he could patch. This thought moved him to add
to this part of his inventory his blanket roll—two very
ancient blankets, a torn sheet, a polyethylene garment
bag and the five feet of clothesline they were tied up
with—and his belt, plus a spool of heavy-duty thread
with a veritable whaler's needle stuck into it, an old
single-edged razor blade, and the canvas floor covering
of the crate. Oh, yes, his Scout knife, too—it had an
awl in it, which would pierce canvas or leather.

That seemed to cover tailoring and shoemaking.
Nothing could be done now about the fact that he was
totally ignorant of both trades. While the oxygen lasted,
he would have to try to learn.

The notation for vitamins reminded him that he was
going to have to be sick some of the time—or perhaps
even much of the time. But he did not even need to look
into his first-aid kit to know how inadequate it was.
Aspirin, PVP-iodine, Band-Aids, about a dozen capsules
of some antibiotic left over from an illness of two years
ago and hence probably halved in potency, a semi-
squashed tube of anaesthetic ointment; that was all.
Were he to be seriously ill, he would die, and that would
be that. In view of the immediacy of the oxygen problem, the medical one did not alarm him much, however.
Though he was scared, he felt the basic strength of his
youth, and in addition a reassuring doubt that any Martian germ could be a real menace to his Earthborn body.

Good thing he wasn't a girl, at least. What a nuisance
that would have been.

What about equipment—to build a pump, to charge the battery, to construct every possible needed device in the few minutes Mars would probably leave him between noticing the need and finishing the machine? Nothing that he saw in the cabin was reassuring, but he noted every item on the wall all the same: one table; one breadboard rig (with dead tube); a small soldering iron, with solder and flux (if there would be power for it); six Ehrlenmeyer flasks, once intended for specimens; six feet of glass tubing, in three 24-inch lengths; a blowpipe; a glass file; twin tubes of epoxy glue; a small tripod; a roll of friction tape; a coil of copper wire, length unknown, but obviously no more than five feet and probably less; and, *mirabile dictu,* an axe, newly sharpened. In addition—for though they were less obvious, they too were tools—he had two pencils, a ball-point pen, a drawing compass, a protractor, a pocket compass, a wristwatch, a pair of binoculars, two star charts, an ephemeris, and the Pic du Midi map of Mars (the most recent one, revised from the photographs sent back by the unmanned probes).

After a moment's thought, he added to the list of tools a sub-class for Chemicals, but it did not consume much space: the salt, the agar, a small box of lye, six ounces of absolute alcohol and four of formalin. What about his mess kit, and the canteen and canvas sling? Well, call these tools, too; at least, the kit contained a spoon with fork prongs at its end and a cutting edge.

He looked slowly around the cabin, which he had now to begin to think of as his house. He could see nothing that he had missed listing. That meant it was time to empty his pockets, which he did on preposition to the table which bore the dead rig. When he was through he had a bandanna; an extra pair of rawhide shoelaces; a pocket notebook; a few loose coins (to call home with?); his matches (in, ironically, a waterproof case); his wallet, containing four dollars and assorted cards (plus a snapshot of Nanette in the patented secret compartment); a key-ring on a snake chain with eleven keys on it, all of them now as useless as six of them had always been mysterious; and finally, his class ring (which he had almost given to Nanette, and might just

as well have, for all the good it was likely to do him on
Mars).

And that was absolutely all. No, not quite. There
were eight small paper-clips and one middle-sized one
marking pages in the ephemeris; and thrust into the
wall, holding up the charts and the Pic du Midi map,
fourteen push-pins.

No matter how he looked at it all, it was not much
of a survival kit. For anything else, he would have to
depend upon Mars—and upon luck, who had abruptly
already stopped smiling on him.

What now? Think!

But he could think of nothing, except that he was
suddenly and violently thirsty.

When the goddess of luck stops smiling, she is often
likely to be thorough. Although Dolph had no way of
knowing it, when she had run out on him on Mars, she
had simultaneously deserted him forty-eight million
miles away.

Nanette had noticed that the tree-house was miss-
ing, on the very morning of its departure.

Though she had taken sporadic care to disguise it
around Dolph, Nanette's mind was quick as well as
gifted, and relentlessly logical as only the feminine mind
can be without formal training. In addition, she had a
strong visual imagination—so powerful, in fact, that
she was still wavering between wanting to be a painter,
her first dream, and to be a scientist, a notion sparked
by Dolph—and that midnight trip into the silent skies
in Dolph's first test crate—had put her emotions into
a secret ferment she had hardly been able to confess
even to herself.

It would have taken a dull brain indeed to have failed
to respond to the moonlit wonders of that silent ascent,
and since she already knew in general the vastness of
the problem. Dolph had been nibbling at, she had not
been slow to imagine what an audacious mind might do
with a solution for it—a solution that Dolph obviously
now had, at least in large part. If anti-gravity was
achievable at all, ninety per cent of the work was done—
everything else was technicalities, to be worked out in

detail by any dim-witted engineer, or maybe even by a
household electrician.

And now the tree-house was gone—and not a footprint below it to show that it had been carried anyplace
else on Earth. It had been an elaborate and heavy tree-
house; it couldn't possibly have been just wafted away—
unless, of course, it had done precisely and only that.
It could not have vanished in any other way but that.

She questioned Dolph's mother cautiously. That was
difficult, for the two women liked each other, and it
was impossible for Nanette to disguise the fact that she
was troubled. Luckily, Dolph's cover story was good
enough to give her reason to be troubled; had he really
gone camping without even letting her know he was
going, she would have had good reason to be furious,
and Mrs. Haertel drew that conclusion and commiser-
ated with her on male thoughtlessness. Nanette with-
drew unscathed but shaky, and now furious indeed,
though for quite different reasons.

Given the additional facts in her possession, she saw
at once that the cover story was full of holes, and only
a little more elementary detective work among the tools,
scraps, shavings and last-minute discards that Dolph
had left was enough to confirm the conclusion she had
been trying all morning not to have to draw.

She climbed into the loft-space of the garage and
hunkered down in the only part of it that had a floor,
a dark and filthy corner where Dolph—years earlier,
before they had met—had abortively kept pigeons, all
of which had died of some fungus disease Mrs. Haertel
had said was dangerous to people. too.

"The bum," Nanette said bitterly. "That steaming,
no-good, sneaky, runaway bum."

She was not at all surprised to find herself crying.
She did a thorough job of it, though silently enough so
that someone passing the garage would have heard from
the abandoned cote only an occasional, ghostly coo. When
it was over, half an hour later, she felt quite washed
out—still furious, to be sure, but ready to cope with
male perfidy on any scale the situation required. Wip-
ing her nose on the inadequate tail of her shirt, she

crunched back down the unsafe stairs to examine, first, Dolph's work-bench, and then the abandoned test crate.

"The bum," she told the test crate.

"I'll show *him*," she said, poking at half a bucket of glass-hard pitch.

"Run out on me, will he," she growled at an uncrumpled wiring diagram from the waste can.

"And besides," she said to last year's ephemeris, "he's sure to be in trouble."

With an unexpected and uncontrollably loud sniffle, Nanette strode toward home in search of a soldering iron, constructing in her head as she went the rudiments of a cover story for herself. Though she had never before needed a really good one, she was grimly confident that she could make a better job of it than Dolph had: constructing cover stories, and passing them off with a perfectly bland countenance, is another of the instinctive feminine arts for which no practice is needed (though sometimes it helps).

It was not Nanette's fault that this story—for her, for Dolph, and for all the world—needed to be longer, wilder and more portentous than any told since the Viking longboats groped toward an unknown Greenland. After all, she was only trying to nail down her man, with the same weapons that had served women beside the brooks of Swanscombe in 250,000 B.C.

"You in-ter-plan-e-tary *hobo*," she muttered across 48 million miles of storming space. "I'll show *you*."

5. MORNING ON MARS

Dolph awoke slowly, stiff with cold and with the hard boards under his blankets. His mouth was parched, his lips cracked, his lungs wheezing. He felt half suffocated; and when he sat up, with a great start of alarm, he became so dizzy that he fell back with a gasp, wondering where he was and what was wrong with him.

Then he remembered. Without sitting up, he looked about cautiously. A hard beam of bluish sunlight, as sharp and merciless as a laser ray, struck horizontally across the cabin from the porthole but did not seem to reflect off anything; the rest of the enclosure was as dim as a cave. He tasted his dry lips with a swollen tongue, which made him cough, and at once he became conscious of being embedded in an enormous silence; even the cough sounded remote and feeble in his own ears, and when the silence flowed back it was as enormous as the bottom of the sea. Now he realized what had awakened him: a non-noise—the end of the last hiss of his first oxygen bottle.

He struggled to his feet. The dizziness returned, but it was not as severe this time, and slowly passed. He

51

wondered if he should worry about it, but he was almost
certain that it was an effect of gravity—after all, he
weighted only forty-eight pounds here, and it would
take his heart and blood vessels time to get used to the
lightened load.

Oxygen was what counted now. He could allow time
for nothing else until that need was met. And he had
to face the fact that he would have to consume a good
deal to provide for the possibility of more. He cracked
open the second flask and got to work.

First of all he ate, and then, from the traces of fat
left in the K-ration container and a few crystals of lye,
he made a weak soap solution. A small loop of wire
gave him a passable bubble-pipe, and with the floating
bubbles he had no trouble in locating three leaks in the
walls of his cabin, two of them large enough to be critical. He marked them. There was bound to be minor
seepage too, but he could worry about that later, when
the interior pressure was high enough to make detect-
ing it possible.

Next, an electric motor. That was a simple enough
proposition, required only two bits of metal and some
wire, plus a frame which he delayed building until he
could be absolutely sure of how he wanted to use the
machine. He was already sure that the motor itself was
too small, no matter how he would want to use it; but
it was as big as he dared to build it with what he had
on hand, and that would have to be that.

For now, he wanted it as the heart of a pump, of a
simple design he remembered seeing once in an adver-
tisement in a technical magazine. It was a pump that
would never get wet, no matter what it pumped, because it consisted of nothing but two rollers continu-
ously squeezing a few inches of soft rubber tubing. The
input end would go through the largest of his leaks to
the Martian atmosphere; the output would open into
the cabin.

But what was he going to do for rollers? That was
easy—two brief lengths of glass tubing, fused on to
nails as axles with the aid of the Sterno can and the
blowpipe. But he had to turn up the oxygen even more
to get the Sterno to burn at all, and even so, his air

was almost pure poison by the time the operation was done. At home it would not have cost him half an hour; here, it was as hard work as heaving coal.

At last, however, the motor was connected to the battery, and humming fairly smoothly. The little poot-poots of air that came out of it could hardly be felt, but he could only hope that they would add up to a sizable increase in pressure before too long. He had used the Sterno heat simultaneously to soften a gob of pitch, with which he now closed the remaining leaks in the hull. Then, after five minutes of rest—it was not nearly enough—he valved the oxygen back down to a trickle.

While he rested, he became conscious of a kind of whispering, which at first he could not identify. Then he thought it might be wind, although such a thing seemed impossible in the near-vacuum outside. Or was it? After all, many an astronomer had seen sandstorms sweeping Mars—seen them, and often cursed them for obscuring the view at a crucial opposition. Dolph got up and peered out.

It was wind, all right. Gentle, almost imperceptible waves were moving along the surface of the ground-clinging vegetation, which as he watched became obscured by a faint haze, as though some invisible housekeeper were dusting them.

After only a few moments, the whispering had become a sighing, and then the sighing developed a soft but definite whistling edge around the packing-crate. The haze rose, and the near wall of the crater began to become dim. Soon it had vanished completely, and the air had become quite dark; though it was still obviously day, there was no longer any direct sunlight visible—it was as though the sky had become overcast. For a wild moment, Dolph wondered if it were going to rain.

But of course it didn't. The air simply continued to become darker with flying dust and fine sand. It was a good thing that his pump design didn't allow any access of the air to its moving parts, for the machine was far too fragile to stand much abrasion. As it was, he'd do well to clap some kind of filter over its input hole— and change the filter daily, if this kind of flurry happened every morning.

If this was just part of a general sandstorm, of course, the story was over; he would be buried, and that would be that.

In half an hour, however, the whistling began to abate, and the day began to seem lighter once more. By the end of an hour, the crater was as still and brilliant as it had ever been; the thin air couldn't carry even impalpable dust long without any current to keep it in motion. The whole thing, Dolph supposed, was just a local gust, probably caused by the heating of the valley when the sunlight struck it after the Hyperboreal night.

He hoped so; for if the little storm were a regular occurrence, he could use it; in fact, it would solve one of his most pressing problems—the problem of how to keep his batteries charged. There was power for the taking out there. All he had to do was build a small generator—a slightly larger version of his motor, with a magnetized piece of steel for a rotor, would do nicely— and a windmill. He could probably cut the sails for the windmill from his canvas; the stuff was rather heavy for the thin air, but on the other hand the gusts seemed to have plenty of energy behind them. Only experiment would decide what the best sail design would be, though.

His watch said that it was now near noon; the sun didn't agree. The disagreement would grow as the slightly longer Martian day expanded, and as more days followed. He could of course open the back of the watch and retard the mechanism's governor as far as it would go, but he doubted that it would prove to be enough. It would be better to keep Martian time, approximately, and use the watch only for timing short operations, as the need arose... and not risk exposing the watch's innards to the dryness and the dust. Its sealed interior probably still preserved something quite close to an Earth-normal atmosphere, and he decided against sacrificing that for an experiment in collimation which was probably too delicate to come off anyhow.

But the reminder of noon reminded him also that at home he would be coming up on lunch-time. Here on Mars, he would have to give it another title: No-lunch time, or perhaps some title that didn't mention food at all. Medieval man, after all, had got along handily on two meals a day, and animals—carnivores, anyhow—only had to be fed once. Until further notice, he was going to have to be an animal. All the same, if he had, say, a stack of blueberry pancakes about seven inches high, and a pitcher of cold buttermilk, and...

No more of *that* nonsense, he told himself grimly. You get six ounces of water—and then back to work.

What was next? Potentially, he had air pressure; and, even more potentially, he had power. But he still did not have oxygen—only a means of conserving it slightly, not of replenishing it. He had to have a source.

Was the clear fluid in the Martian plants water—or something that was mostly water? If so, that would solve his oxygen problem too, if he kept busy enough, for he could always crack it by electrolysis—and burn the hydrogen produced after the Sterno ran out, if he could figure out a way to store the hydrogen. He seriously doubted that he could, for the universe's lightest gas is elusive stuff even under Earth-normal pressures, and he certainly couldn't hope to pump it successfully through rubber tubing—you might as well hope to pump water through tubing made of sponge.

He shook his head savagely. Hydrogen wasn't his problem. The thinness and impoverishment of the air was blurring his thinking—that, and the fact that he was hungry, though as yet the hunger was probably mostly in his imagination. Oxygen was what he needed—not hydrogen, oxygen!

He opened one of his specimen bottles cautiously and looked at the ambiguous plants inside it. They did not seem much withered; well, maybe the denser, damper air inside the cabin was a feast to them. The little transparent sacs were stiff and glistening, as though they were nearly ready to burst. How to tell if that stuff was water?

He popped one experimentally. To his intense disappointment, nothing came out of it—nothing at all. Inside it was bone dry. He popped another, with the same result. If the sacs didn't store sap, then what could they be for?

While he was puzzling about that, he pinched another sac, which promptly confused him by spurting cold liquid into his face, in a fine spray which dried instantly and left him feeling sticky and taut, as though he had just dried off after coming out of the ocean. No doubt about that one—that had been sap of some sort, containing salts in solution, and probably sugars, too. But what was the solvent?

He still could think of no simple chemical test which might answer this question. Yet, after all, what other answer could there be? There is only one universal solvent—or at least, only one which is stable at the temperature ranges prevalent on Mars. On Jupiter, liquid ammonia might do nicely—but luckily, he wasn't on Jupiter. Mars was quite bad enough. It had to be water. It just couldn't be anything else.

What about the substances that were dissolved in it? They might well be poisonous. He didn't dare take the chance that they weren't—at least, not yet, not until his food ran out. He would have to distill the sap after he had collected it—more heat needed for that, but perhaps not heat which would consume oxygen; he might power a still from the sun, with an arrangement of burning glasses and mirrors. Come to think of it, a simple mirror arrangement might help to warm the cabin during the day, too.

Speaking of the sun, what had happened to it? The cabin was getting dark again. Automatically, he looked at his watch: 4:38. He had been on Mars just a little past one full Earth day. It would not be dusk yet up on the tilted plateau—only midafternoon—but the floor of the oasis would get no more direct sunlight today, and the temperature would already be dropping. Would there be another brief sandstorm shortly after full dark? Probably—but with luck he would sleep through it.

With luck he would sleep through a great deal more than that.

In general, the less activity the better, beyond what was absolutely necessary to keep himself alive until—

Until what?

He discovered that he did not know. Rescue was out of the question; just to begin with, nobody knew where he was. He supposed it would be possible, once his windmill-generator was set up, to build a spark-gap radio transmitter and to make it heard, for he remembered having read somewhere that the amount of power required for effective interplanetary radio was astonishingly small. But that would do him precisely no good at all, for a spark-gap transmitter can send nothing but bursts of noise—dots and dashes, long noises and short ones—and he did not know any code, Morse or otherwise, except, ironically, . . . -- . . . for "help!" and . . .- from the Beethoven Fifth Symphony, which his foster-father somehow knew was Morse for "v"—also useless.

In fact, the spark would do him no good until the first manned formal expedition to Mars was actually in the sky above him. Then he could use it to draw attention to himself, and, come to think of it, the expedition could triangulate on the signal and locate him precisely. Until then, he had many better uses for electricity than producing arbitrarily patterned bursts of radio noise.

And the first manned formal expedition to Mars was a long way off yet—a *long* way off. At the thought, he sat down on the floor and began to batter one fist slowly, mechanically into the palm of the other hand. Up until now, when he had considered the matter of survival at all except on the minute-to-minute basis of actually working at it, he had thought in terms of months. But survival *and rescue?* That was going to be a matter of years . . . and, perhaps, a matter of decades.

No stretching of rations would carry him through that. If he lived at all, he was going to have to live off the land—off the most alien, the most bitter, the most inhospitable land ever to feel the impact of a human foot.

If only he had thought to bring a spare tube—the *only* component in the breadboard rig whose failure could not be compensated for by any sort of improvisation! If only, in general—since in fairness to himself he would not have asked anyone's forethought to be quite so specific—it had occurred to him that *something,* no matter what, might happen to make his stay longer than his plans had called for! There were twenty

small articles he might have brought with him, all
without overloading his craft in the least, that would
have increased his chances of survival many times over
twenty-fold.

But it was too late now. He was on Mars for ten
years to come, and quite possibly for life.

Suddenly he realized that it was pitch black in the
crate. Where had the day gone? He hadn't accomplished
a fraction of what needed to be done.

In the darkness he could hear his air-pump running.
For a moment the sound was obscurely comforting—
at least he had got that much done—until he noticed
that the pump's cycle seemed to have developed a slight
irregularity; he'd have to check that, first thing in the
morning. Quite possibly there was some grit lodged
somewhere in the tubing which was throwing the thing
off stride. If the obstruction got any bigger it might
break one of the glass rollers.

In the meantime, through the cold blackness of the
Martian night it whispered to him steadily:

Forlife forlife forlife forlife forlife forlife forlife...

PART TWO

Friday

6. EVENING ON MARS

It was not strictly true, of course, that no one knew where Dolph was. But for all the good it did him—or was going to do him in the foreseeable future—it might just as well have been true.

Nanette now knew where he was with some specificity. A discarded map of Mars torn out of a book—discarded apparently because it was a Flagstaff map, out of an observatory where astronomers had been letting their imaginations abet their eyes about the red planet ever since the days of Lowell—a scribbled ellipse enclosed the Sinus Sabaeus; and common sense told her that Dolph would most likely have stuck to that planned landing area, simply because so large a green spot, so near the equator, would be almost guaranteed to be among the most livable areas on Mars, particularly in high summer. That the marked area was at least as big as Florida did not daunt her at all, since it never occurred to her; even more than Dolph—probably because she was younger—her thought processes were a mixture of sheer brass, naïve and hence astounding ingenuity, and glorious inattention to niggling but cru-

cial details which would have scared any adult green—
any adult, that is, who like most could no longer recall
the contradictions that had made up his own brain as
a teenager.

Nanette also knew, even more specifically, how Dolph
had got where he was, and how she was going to get
there after him. On this latter count, quite a bit of the
work had already been done for her, in the form of
Dolph's first flying model—the one he had taken her
aloft in, thus putting the essence of his secret in her
hands—which still stood on the floor of the garage.
With the aid of the wiring diagrams she had been able
to check the rig—which, being the original, was even
simpler than the one which had actually taken Dolph
away—and, with her soldering iron, to repair the few
places in the circuit Dolph's voltmeter showed had failed,
or might fail under a work load. The bucket of pitch
had suggested to her the necessity of caulking her proposed craft (she might, it must be confessed, not have
thought of it without some such hint), and in general,
once she knew the category in which she needed to be
thinking, other clues, hints and helps popped out at her
not only from all over the garage, but from memory
and from reading, in bewildering profusion.

She could not take advantage of all of them. For one
thing, she was dead certain that she was in a hurry—
and even under normal circumstances she was not much
inclined to be patient. Second, she had not accumulated
any money for the venture, and even at the best would
have had fewer sources to call upon than Dolph had
had. Finally—and most crucially—she did not think
of everything.

But in one major respect, she kept her head: she left
a note. It read:

Dear Mum and Dad, and Mr. & Mrs. Haertel,

You won't believe this but you simply must, because
it's absolutely true. Dolph has not gone camping. He
has gone to Mars, and I have gone after him.

I know how this sounds but maybe if we do not come
back for a while and you don't find us anywhere else

you may think of it again. We haven't eloped or run
away or anything stupid like that. It's just that Dolph
has discovered some kind of antigravity which is *very*
simple to build and run. He took me for a short run in
it and then he built a sort of spaceship in his tree-house
and went to Mars in it on a junket. I know he didn't
plan to stay long because he didn't take enough supplies
and things with him, but he's not back yet and I have
to go because he probably needs help.

He marked a place called Sinus Sabaeus on a map
of Mars and I'm pretty sure he's stuck somewhere there,
so that's where I'm going too. I will bring him back if
everything goes right. If it doesn't then we really will
be in a pickle, but please don't worry.

.   Love and things, NANETTE

She carefully enclosed the map in the envelope—but
none of Dolph's wiring diagrams, or his calculations, or
his notes, or anything else that might have helped anyone to re-discover Dolph's anti-gravity, let alone put it
immediately to useful work. All these she packed neatly
into a manila envelope for Dolph, on the chance—which
she thought good—that he might have left some one
of them behind by accident, and would now be needing
it.

Then she heaved and tugged her own small vessel
on to an old sled, hauled it out of the garage into the
road, and took off—in darkness, as Dolph had gone.
With her went the priceless and useless envelope of
papers—useless to Dolph, and certainly to her; and
priceless because, left on Earth, they would have been
Dolph's and Nanette's last hope of rescue. The darkness
swallowed her with its usual indifference, leaving behind only the heart-stopping, icy flame of a summer
night in Iowa, where hardly anyone ever looks up at
the eternal stars except the young who love them.

As for Dolph, he was making a wine-press, and finding
it a harder job than his preliminary sketches had made
it seem. Had he had nothing but grapes to think about,

he would have given it up at once; but it was his own
life he was trying to squeeze.

He had yet to discover what else besides water was
in the sap-sacs of the tumble-lichens; but when the fiery,
itching dryness of his mouth, throat and nose in the
mornings was complemented by nose-bleeds and a
hacking cough, he realized belatedly that he had to keep
his cabin air moist, or die of dehydration of the respi-
ratory system. A wick of torn cloth dipped into a Petri
dish seemed the logical answer to that—and yet he
hated to use his bottled water for any purpose besides
actually drinking it.

The obvious solution was to use sap squeezed out of
the plants. There was a dividend of sorts to be gained
in the process, too. In the course of aimlessly popping
the apparently empty sacs and wondering what they
contained, and what they were good for if the answer
was "Nothing," he had thought to pop one near a match-
flame. The match had produced a brief, tiny, but quite
definite increase in brightness. The "empty" sacs, in
short, contained oxygen—perhaps not the pure stuff,
but close to it.

Both discoveries made sense. There was not enough
water vapor or oxygen in the Martian atmosphere to
sustain a plant so much like an Earthly one as this was.
The tumble-lichen obviously had to crack both out of
the basic limonite sands in which it grew. And to maintain sufficient vapor pressure and oxygen tension to
support life in its cells, it had to maintain both inside
itself—in that part of the environment the famous
physiologist Claude Bernard had called the *milieu in-
terieur*—since both were denied it on the outside.

Hence if Dolph were to squeeze water out of the plants
inside his cabin, he would pick up a little oxygen too—
probably no more than a small fraction of what he
needed, but every extra molecule was a gain. The cake
that was left over after the pressing operation could be
piled outside the packing-crate, against the time when
he might need it for bedding, for insulation, for fertilizer—he really had no idea what it might eventually
be good for. He did already know, however, that for him
the first law of survival was, *Save it*—no matter what

"it" might be. (And many New Englanders might have told him the second and third laws, which were *Use it up* and *Make it do;* but he had in fact already arrived at them, although he hadn't put them to himself quite so tersely.)

When the wine-press was completed, it looked quite like a bellows-frame without its collapsible sides (or what a health-food addict would have called a juicer). The next step he had planned was to begin to make a still from some of his available glassware, while he still had enough oxygen to insure finishing the job—and before time had insured that he would need yet more oxygen to complete it, by providing accidents to break some of the glassware.

But the day was already waning—he had long since given up believing that Martian days were actually longer than Earth days—and he did not want to break off making the still in the middle. Instead, it seemed like a useful idea to give the press a try. That would take him outside to gather tumble-lichens. He had not been outside for two days, and needed the exercise before he became both too stiff and too weak to move. The cramped quarters, the cold nights and the low gravity were all conspiring to rob him of strength and mobility.

He attached to his belt a length of clothesline to bale up the plants with, donned his heavy clothes and his respirator, and crawled out on to the powdery sands. He was just in time for the evening dust-up, which nearly froze him before he could get out into the lee of his ship, but it was quickly over and seemed to have done him no permanent damage. He resolved, nevertheless, to check on how close dusk might be before venturing outside again; there would be no harvesting for him this evening.

Before starting back, he indulged himself in a glance at the sky. It was quite black at the zenith and almost all the way to the horizons, though there was a remaining glow of steel blue along the edge of the crater behind which the small sun had set. The stars were brilliant, and there seemed to be thousands of them, many more than had ever been visible in the Iowa skies even during the best conditions of seeing; he doubted

that Mars would ever allow him the time to relearn to
pick out the constellations, although their shapes could
not be much changed here. They would be swamped out
by the vast number of "new" stars masked by Earth's
atmosphere.

All the same, there were two unusual objects in the
sky right now. One was a dim spark of light skimming
over the northern edge of the crater. It had to be one
of the two satellites—nothing else in the Martian sky
could move visibly—and of them, the choice was probably Deimos, the larger and farther out of the two; he
was almost surely too far south on the planet to be able
to see Phobos, even from up on the plateau. Even Deimos was only a dim spark, very far removed indeed
from the low-hanging, looming Deimos of Edgar Rice
Burroughs's Mars. Had it not been moving, he would
have been unable to pick it out from many stars more
brilliant.

But the other unusual object was something about
which there could be no argument, though Dolph had
never seen it before in just this way. It was a star as
brilliant as Rigel or Sirius, and—though none of the
Martian stars twinkled, for the atmosphere was far too
thin for that—with a steady intensity which ear-
marked it as not a star at all, but a planet. Furthermore,
though it glared as blue-white as any of the stellar
giants, there was also a greenness about its light shared
by no star Dolph had ever seen, then or now.

Looking up at it, Dolph felt himself slowly drowning
in an invisible sea of homesickness. He would not have
believed it possible that anyone could feel his whole
heart and soul so drawn toward what seemed to be no
more than a point of light... brilliant and beautiful, to
be sure, but only one among so many...

Then the Earth went out.

For the moment he thought his eyes had failed him,
and brushed one glove across his goggles. In the next,
a sudden shocking suspicion of disaster hit him, one of
those nightmares with which everyone had lived since
Hiroshima—but if the Earth had blown up, then—

He was left no time for guessing, for other stars
around where the Earth had been were going out too—

and then, just for a second, there flashed in the black space near the zenith a sort of lozenge of reddish-yellow light, like one side of a falling box.

It *was* a falling box, which had briefly caught the last of the sunlight before sinking below the lip of the crater. Now he could no longer judge its fall except by the spreading area of starlessness above him. It was— it had to be, there was no other possibility—another crate like his own. It was heading straight down for him, and it was coming far too fast.

He knew that it would do him no good to run. He might just as well die under it, as be in the clear if it were going to smash his own home. He stood rooted to the freezing ground, watching.

The area of blackness grew. Then, suddenly, it seemed to stop growing for a moment, and veer off to the north-west. In the next instant, it was no longer between him and the stars, and was lost in the general night.

Then there was nothing. Had he imagined the whole thing? He almost hoped so. He had already guessed what crate the new one had to be—for surely any real attempt at rescuing him would have equipped itself with something bigger, not smaller, than his—and he had, also, a horrified suspicion as to who might be in it. Better a moment of nightmare, brought about by loneliness and oxygen starvation, than that his guesses should turn out to be right—

A long, rending smash tore through the blackness, long seconds after the count-down in his unconscious mind had told him to expect it. Its extraordinary loud-ness in the tenuous air told him that it must be very close. Snarling into his respirator fragments of phrases his foster-father would have whaled him for—though that was probably where they had come from, on some remote occasion when the boy was supposed to be safely out of earshot—Dolph began to run.

7. CHILDREN IN THE SKY

From all the reading Dolph had done in his relatively short life, and from the same amount of observation of people, he had been more than entitled to conclude that any real rescue was years away, if it were ever to come at all. True, most of the people that he had known personally were pleasant people who were far from short either of money or of good will—people who would not hesitate to help someone in trouble if they could, or thought they could. By the same token, most of the fiction he had read had been about fantastically self-centered, unwashed people without a grain of human kindness even towards themselves, who seemed to be distracted from prolonged acts of suicide only to strike out at the people around them. Between the two, he struck a rough sort of balance, and concluded that on Mars, he was on his own.

His knowledge of the state of the art called space-flight, as it had existed at the time he left Earth, was equally rough, but roughly accurate: there was no hope for a really adequate expedition for years to come, even

on a crash basis to rescue him—which he could hardly
hope for. Earth's technology simply wasn't up to it yet.

In all this, he was quite right, but he had left out
one factor, simply because he had never heard of it.
That was not his fault; no example of it had turned up
during his lifetime. It was that factor which newspaper-
men, in their brutal but not always cynical jargon, call
the Baby Down the Well.

To be sure, at first Dolph's and Nanette's parents
had suspected the worst—which, as Nanette had known
automatically, meant an elopement, either with or
without marriage; but time and lack of evidence dis-
posed of that awful notion—time, lack of evidence, and
a creeping willingness to believe that no matter how
they had zigged and zagged in the past, neither Nanette
nor Dolph could have broken with their characters and
their backgrounds so completely and at the same time.
Faith had set in.

The next horrible suspicion was kidnapping and
murder, but no ransom notes arrived, and no bodies
were found. Finally—and with rising despair that any
outsider would have mistaken for self-righteous fury—
the families concluded that the youngsters had simply
gone camping and had lied about it (inventively, out-
rageously, but probably borrowing the fantastic ele-
ments from Something They Had Read) to gain time
for an unusually long trip. But at long last this story,
too, fell to the ground of its own weight, for there was
no evidence for it at all.

During all this time—a matter of weeks—the ground
around both homes was literally strewn with clues which
could point in only one direction: the direction in
which Dolph and Nanette actually had gone, and in
which Nanette had honestly said that they had gone.
Since at bottom what both families wanted most in all
the world was to have their children back safe and
whole, they were finally left with no recourse but to
believe in the only evidence, as well as in the honesty
of their children.

It took a long time, for none of the adults had any
better opinion than Dolph had of how the authorities
would greet such a story. But the time the families had

taken to mull over the alternatives in private both stood
in their favor, and drove them out of themselves. They
had done their best, with their own limited resources
and that of the local police. Now they *had* to do more;
and they did not stint. They sent telegrams to their
senators and representatives; they appealed to the
President and to N.A.S.A. big-wigs both in Washington
and at Cape Kennedy; they made long-distance tele-
phone calls to scientists in the space program; they
pulled wires; and—most courageously of all—they
talked, without pulling any punches, to the Press.

The Press had heard it all, and cried Hoax. To the
papers and to television alike, it was only another Silly
Season story, like the previous decade's obsession with
flying saucers—something to fill up space during a hot
summer, while important news tends to be slow in coming through because most of the world's movers and
shakers are on vacation, and most readers and viewers
are too fagged with the post-vacation blues to care
whether what they are told is an important piece of
news or an obvious piece of nonsense. During the Silly
Season, what both the Press and the public most wants
is someone to make fun of, to feel superior to—providing that it isn't too much work. The two desperate Iowa
families filled the bill nicely, and got the full treatment.
Their nights were filled with despair; their days, with
impotent rage.

But not even the Silly Season lasts forever, and here
and there several important people had already listened to the two families and had taken them seriously—or had stopped to think what it might mean to
the space program if they were taken seriously. In
Washington, somebody high up in N.A.S.A. who knows
Mrs. Haertel spoke soberly to somebody even higher,
and slow machineries began to awaken from their summer sleeps. A mathematician in London who had been
a renegade from Relativity all his life read the garbled
newspaper stories, covered eighteen pages of foolscap
with calculations only two other men in the world could
have any hope of following, and sent them by ordinary
post to one of those men. His assistant prudently photographed the calculations before they were enveloped

and sent the negatives, hidden under a postage stamp, to Moscow, where the other man was. (There are many different kinds of renegades in the world, and they do not always know when they are working together.) The man in Moscow brooded over them for a long and dreadful night, and decided to risk his life, his career, his family and even his country on them—though perhaps not exactly in that order. The lonely operator of a 68-foot radio telescope in the Australian outback focused his gigantic dish-shaped antenna on Mars and picked up, from he could not tell where on that remote desert, traces of a signal which might have come from a small but heavily sparking electric motor, and began to compose a brief technical paper to be called "Irregular Broad-Spectrum Martian Probability Anomalies" for a journal called (in Latin) *Proceedings of the Swiss Society for the Freedom of the Ether*, which in consequence would not be seen by anybody likely to be interested in it for decades to come. There was more—most of it not known of at the time, and much of it still hidden in obscure files all over the world, some of it out of secrecy, some out of simple ignorance—but all of it working, however slowly and marginally, in the same direction.

And less slowly, because the pressures on it were greater, the Press found the Silly Season over, and the story still standing . . . not only alive and unrefuted, but showing some signs of official interest, of being after all important. The Press made inquiries of the appropriate officials, but was rebuffed without comment; this only made the story seem more likely to be important, after all. And with nothing official to go on, the Press was driven back to re-discovering the Baby Down the Well. The Press handled it like this:

CHILDREN LOST IN SKY, N.A.S.A. HINTS
Space Scientist's son,
Girl-Friend Stuck on Mars?
Sen. Hill, Committee Demand End to Secrecy on Mars
Teen Flyaways Rumored
Doomed on Red Planet;
U.S.S.R. May Plot Mercy Trip

"Save Our Kids"; Mars Parents' Own Story

MARS TOTS MYTH, RED SCOFFS

Shiela Djarling Talks to Teens:
"HONEYMOON ON MARS—REAL GOFFIN, PREACH!"

Hill committee Seeks Untold Mars History

SPACE SCIENTIST SAYS: MARS KIDS DEAD

HHH ORDERS CRASH MARS RESCUE
Cape Kennedy Scientists
Seek Ways to Speed
"Project Ares" Flagship

The world was indeed fully as bad a place as Dolph had assessed it to be—indeed worse, for his memory encompassed no important war—but all the same, let one Baby fall down a Well, and all the resources of technology are mustered to save it, while the rest of humanity, on the spot in spirit and passionately applying body-English from the sidelines like rooters at a billiards tournament, hangs upon the half-hourly bulletins from the Press.

Well-intentioned but stupid people sent the two anxious families money. Others turned up in droves simply to gape at their homes, or—until police cordons stopped it—to cut or dig souvenirs. More interviews were sought than the families could have granted even in a twenty-four hour day devoted to nothing else. Thousands of persons who had never looked at the sky before in their lives could now point to where they thought Mars was, and it was astonishing how many times they were right; and a quasi-mystical hobby called "the Mars vigil" captured a number of minor religious sects, especially in southern California (where the fact that Mars was a red planet also convinced some of the politically religious that the Children in the Sky were just more parts of the great Communist Plot, along with U.N.I.C.E.F. and mixed marriages)—in addition, of course, to the uncountable number of prayers offered in all the major churches of the world.

But the element which gives the Baby Down the Well its suspense is the knowledge, lurking always at the back of everyone's mind, that there must soon come a time after which all the effort and all the hope will have been for nothing. Detective work far more thorough and scientific than any the families could even have engaged, let alone paid for, soon established within quite small limits of error what supplies Dolph and Nanette had taken with them—and therefore, the maximum time they could be expected to stay alive, assuming (for the sake of hope) that they had both landed on Mars gently and without any hurt, loss or damage. It was immediately evident that the *von Braun*, the Ares Project's flagship, could not be completed within that time—let alone launched upon a crossing it would then take the ship 228 days to make.

(This fact, however, in no way discouraged the newspapers from sponsoring bus trips by high school science clubs to Cape Kennedy to watch the *von Braun* being built—though there was very little to be seen from the distances over which the trippers had to look even after they reached their destination. The trippers themselves made fine copy—almost as good as candid-camera or man-on-the-street interviews. The television networks agreed.)

And no amount of detective work, nor scientific research either solo or in conference, did better than approach the margins of the discovery by which Dolph and Nanette had made the trip. This fact alone increased the urgency to rescue the youngsters to a pitch almost as high among scientists as it was in the families—not only because the knowledge was wanted, but because the scientists suspected in Dolph a mind of a caliber not seen on Earth since the death of Norbert Weiner, or perhaps even the immortal Hermann Weyl. After all, Dolph had made the discovery which the scientists could not—and could not even with the most important fact in their possession, a fact that Dolph hadn't had: that the thing could be done, and had been done.

The time ran out, inexorably. Toward the end, the *New York Times* began to post in Times Square the number of days the youngsters had left, and then, the number of hours. For the last day of all, the *Times* put up the red ball impaled upon a pole, the fall of which usually indicated nothing more momentous than the election of someone to the presidency of the United States. This time, its fall would mark the expiration of the last calculated moment of life for the Children in the Sky.

The ball fell at 11:32 p.m. Eastern Daylight Time, twenty-nine days after Dolph had left the Earth. A huge, silent crowd had gathered to watch, and with its falling, there was a concerted sigh—almost a whisper as it left individual lips, but magnified by numbers into a sort of wave-like moan.

For the rest of that month, flags flew at half-mast all over the world, and no one can estimate how many millions watched the televised memorial services.

Then the flags returned to their usual positions, and the production of memorial books and pamphlets—and souvenirs—began. With the coming of autumn, the serious business of running the world began to come back into the headlines.

The case of the Children in the Sky was over.

Dolph must have reached Nanette within six or seven seconds after the crash, though to him it seemed an eternity of running and searching. The impact had reduced her crate to a jumble of planking and other, more anonymous, debris, but the Martian starlight was more than bright enough for him to see her inert body under the rubble.

He wasted no time. Snatching off his respirator, he clapped it over her face, secured it, and heaved her up out of the wreckage by the shoulders. If it had taken him an eternity to get to her, there was no word for how long it seemed to take him to drag her back, through the bitter, blasting cold in which he could no longer even breathe—let alone dare to gasp—to the dubious haven of his own craft. Bundling her awkward, un-cooperative form through his airlock was also madden-

ingly time-consuming; by now his head was swimming.
But somehow, he got them both inside. Then he just
sat and panted.

He had, after all, gone out for exercise. But this much
had almost been fatal.

After a while, however, he had recovered enough to
take a look at the girl. She was in bad shape. To begin
with, she was so blue with cold, and probably with oxygen starvation, that he could not tell where her blue-
ness was also due to bruises—as a lot of it surely was.
That landing had been hard. If she also had broken
bones, or even more serious injuries, he would be unable
to guess at them until she recovered consciousness and
became able to tell him where and how she hurt worst.

For the time being, there was nothing he could do
but keep feeding her pure oxygen through the mask,
and try to warm her up. For the last purpose, the blanket alone wouldn't do. Without a single second thought,
he crawled under it with her.

It was more than a little like bedding down with an
extra-large rubber ice-bag. Nevertheless, toward
morning, just before dawn, she seemed to be warmer,
and Dolph, who was very cold, managed to sleep a little.
He was awakened again by the morning sandstorm;
and afterwards, Nanette stirred a little, and muttered
something unintelligible underneath the oxygen mask.

Dolph got up promptly, removed the mask and shut
off the oxygen. Then, with creaking muscles, he set
about making a meager breakfast. Nanette, now looking normally pink except for a magnificent black eye,
continued to snooze peacefully, and he did his best not
to disturb her. She needed the sleep—and he needed
more time to think.

For him, it was very clear, the case of the Children
in the Sky was very far from over.

8. WINE AND STORM

Except for the black eye, and a few other, more extensive bruises whose location Nanette refused to specify, there turned out to be nothing wrong with her that oxygen and warmth would not cure—but it had been a near thing. Her crate had leaked enthusiastically during her crossing to Mars, so that she had lost consciousness while still trying to land. That was what had caused the crash, which luckily had been due solely to a short fall under Mars's weak gravity, not to any still-uncanceled momentum.

It was still possible, of course, that she had also got a severe radiation dose during her crossing. But as the days went by without her losing any hair, turning pale, or developing any nausea, Dolph decided to discount that. Except for the bruises, she was almost glaringly healthy—and hungry.

"Well, did you bring any food?" he demanded.

"As much as I could pack into my ship. Remember, it was smaller than yours."

"Meaning that I'm going to have to split with you," Dolph said. "And that probably goes for oxygen and everything else, too. Wuff! Nan, it was nice of you to come after me—and darned smart, too—but we're in a spot. You shouldn't have done it."

"I'm here," Nanette said practically. "And I'm willing to learn—and cooperate. If it helps, I'm sorry I didn't give your notes on the anti-gravity to somebody, and sorry I didn't think ahead about a lot of other things, too. But I didn't, and here I am."

"O.K.—O.K. Now we have to stay alive. I guess the next thing to do is look through that crash of yours and see what we can salvage."

"Good! Let's go."

"Not so fast! And, Nan—try not to *bounce* so. It wastes oxygen. Believe me, we've got to think about every move here before we make it."

"I'm sorry," Nanette said, so instantly contrite that Dolph felt like thirty-three different kinds of heel. "I'll wait for orders."

"It's not a matter of orders," Dolph said, and then had to stop and wonder just how to explain to this burstingly alive girl that she might die any minute and in any one of hundreds of ways—as she almost had several times already. "The first thing is, I've got only one mask, and only one set of heavy clothes, and only one pair of goggles. You don't dare go outside without those things. Outside is—well, it's like the worst features of the top of Mount Everest, plus the worst of a salt desert like Muroc Dry Lake. It's warm enough around noon, but except for that, it's deadly."

"But I already knew that," Nan said in some surprise. "I brought goggles and a mask—I just didn't think to put them on while I was landing. They're out in the wreck, along with my oxygen bottles and my sewing kit."

"Oh. Well, I'll have to go and get them myself. If they're all right, after that we can probably go out together."

"Fine," Nanette said. "While you're gone, I'll make breakfast."

"No, no!"

"*Now* what's the matter?"

Again Dolph had to swallow and start over. "We've

already *had* breakfast, Nan—and lunch and dinner, too. One meal a day is the rule here. And no cooking; while it lasts, we eat the stuff as it comes out of the can. Luckily those field rations heat themselves when you open them, and we can use any extra heat we get. Don't waste any by trying to dress things up. We just can't afford it."

For a moment Nanette looked as though she were about to frown, but instead, she smiled slightly. "All right, I'll forget cooking. Maybe I'll dust—no, I guess that comes under the head of bouncing. Well, at least I won't have to worry about dieting; back home I was getting kind of pudgy."

She paused, looked at Dolph critically, and then laughed outright.

"You look like a dog trying to figure out a porcupine! Go ahead, Dolph. I'm human, and I'll be all right, really I will."

"That's good," Dolph said doubtfully. The girl was in many ways a bigger problem than Mars was, and one about which he knew far less. But since he had no choice, he dressed and went out anyhow, trying to distract himself by wondering what he would find in the wreckage—and what he would find when he came home.

He did not notice that this was the first time he had called the surviving packing-crate "home."

He was, moreover, totally unprepared for what he found when he did get back. Nanette had found the root of the irregularity in the pump cycle, which had been eluding him for weeks.

"What was it?"

"Nothing to it," she said calmly. "You forgot to oil it, that's all."

"But—what did you oil it with?"

"I rubbed the axle-points against my nose. If I've got to have a greasy nose for the next ten years, I might as well use it for something. Sit down and stop gaping, Dolph, and show me what you salvaged."

It had been too much to hope that Nanette's power tube had survived her crash, and indeed it hadn't. But there was a surprising amount of supplies and tools that had,

and with this plus an additional person the interior of
Dolph's crate changed from being almost intolerably
crowded into being impossible. After thinking the matter over, Dolph evolved a solution which also gave him
a use for some of the lumber from the derelict: a
lean-to.

"I think the best place to build it would be on the
airlock side," he added.

"But why? It'll just be in our way."

"No, it won't, not much, and it just might help to
keep us our way out. Maybe you've noticed that the
sandstorms always blow from west to east—just like
weather on Earth—and the airlock faces north. Some
day we're going to have a really big blow and the sand
might dune up against the airlock. If I put the lean-to
on the north side and put its entrance on the east, we'll
have some protection against being sanded in."

"Makes sense," Nanette admitted at once. "Also it
gives us a longer shadow."

"A what? I mean, sure it does, but what of it?"

"The sand blows almost in a line—horizontally. If
the house is twice as long as it is now, it'll catch twice
as much sand against its front and give you twice as
wide a low-sand lane in the back."

"So it would," Dolph said. "And that might be worth
a lot to us some time. Sharp."

"Thank you."

"In fact if you hadn't been sharp you wouldn't be in
this mess at all," he added. Her slightly smug expression evaporated. "Well, let's get on with it. With what's
left over from the lumber, we can put up a windmill—
I think we're past due for a recharging."

Dolph could not build the new structure to suffi-
ciently close tolerances to caulk it, even had he had
enough extra pitch to do the job. He had to settle for
moving more than half of their possessions into the
shed, which at least gave them noticeably more floor
space in their present living quarters.

The windmill-generator worked well, which embol-
dened Dolph to try at last the production of oxygen by
electrolysis of tumble-lichen sap. This worked too, thus
confirming his theory that the sap was largely water;

but it also confronted them with a problem which he should have anticipated, but hadn't. Once the sap was gone, it left behind a brown, gummy residue which was a prime nuisance to clean out. And once he had his still going—thus also solving the drinking water problem, at least for the foreseeable future—the resin accumulated in that, too.

"It must be good for something," he said thoughtfully.

"To eat," Nanette suggested. Nothing on Mars discommoded her so much as her own stomach.

"I'd hate to try it. If the chinks in the lean-to weren't so big I'd try it for caulking."

"Stuff them with dried lichen cake. We've got bales of the stuff outside, even allowing for what blows away."

"It won't pack solid enough. But maybe . . . hmm. You know, I'll bet that if we shredded it fine enough, and used this goo for a binder, it might make passable paper."

"Goody," Nanette said with heavy irony. "Then we can keep a diary."

It was remarkable how Nanette's presence cheered him, no matter how she complicated his problems—or perhaps it was not so remarkable after all.

"But I was still thinking about caulking. We can smooth out the sand in the lean-to for a tray to make the paper in, and turn it out in big sheets—we don't have to care if it isn't uniformly thick—and plaster it up on the walls, as many layers of it as we need. *Then* we can caulk—and pressurize. I'll bet it would take less than a month."

"Better had," Nanette said ambiguously. "Wallpaper on Mars! Well. I vote for a floral pattern."

"Why?"

"Because I'm going to live there, so I get to choose."

"Idiot. Let's go try it."

But her suggestion that the resin might be good to eat continued to work on him, somewhere at the back of his mind. Sooner or later—sooner, now that Nanette was aboard—they were indeed going to have to try the tumble-lichens as food, and pray that they were indeed edible. He decided to attempt the experiment alone and

in private; there was no point in jeopardizing both of
them. When? Not, at least, until after the wall-papering
project was finished. By then, Nanette would have had
enough experience of Mars, and enough warning of the
traps he had encountered before her arrival, to have at
least as good a chance of surviving alone as he would
have had...and a rather better chance than they had
of surviving as a couple.

The obvious need to keep this plan a secret made
facing up to it doubly hard. Somehow he was not helped
by the fact that the wall-papering project was a re-
sounding success, and made Nanette as cheerful as a
puppy at the prospect of having her own quarters. He
wondered if, after all, she wasn't just a little too cheerful, too optimistic about living on Mars, to take the
problems of surviving there alone with enough seri-
ousness. Wouldn't it be better to wait until—

But he recognized this line of reasoning in time as
the excuse it was, and grimly fought it off. When the
appointed moment came, he was not exactly ready to
greet it gladly, but at least he was still determined.

Nanette was in "the next apartment," earnestly pick-
ing up an object from *here* to set it down over *there*—
a feminine rite which these cramped quarters had at
last taught Dolph to appreciate. He was facing about
half an ounce of tumble-lichen sap, freshly squeezed
from the press and hence quite cold. He thought he now
understood, too, how Socrates had felt when faced with
the hemlock. Taking a deep breath, he tossed the swallow down with a most unphilosophic grimace.

Then he held his breath and waited...

The response was not long in coming, and astonished
him completely. Whatever he had expected, it had not
been this. Gradually, but with increasing speed, there
crept through his body a feeling of total well-being. He
was no longer hungry, no longer thirsty, no longer chilly,
no longer even tired. Yet it was more than just an add-
ing up of negatives: he felt strong, alert, as ready for
anything as he had ever felt in his life—and he had
seldom been ill.

He wondered: is this what it's like to be drunk? But
he had experimented with alcohol once, and it had felt

nothing like this. For one thing, alcohol had made him feel happy, almost gay, whereas there did not seem to be any emotional edge to the sensation caused by the sap. For another, alcohol had made him giddy; well, he could test that. He walked across the room and back; no, no dizziness.

He noticed that he was still holding his breath, and let it out. It was several seconds before he realized that he felt no desire to take another. He looked at his watch, and allowed another ten seconds to go by; fifteen; then twenty. He still felt not the slighest need to breathe. A marvelous suspicion smote him and he called out:

"Nanette!"

"What is it? I can barely hear you."

"Come here a minute, will you? Important."

After he called, his diaphragm gave a small heave—just enough, he would guess, to replace the air he had used in calling. Then his chest was quiescent again.

"Dolph—Dolph, what's the matter? You look so strange!"

"How so? I mean, in what way? Do I look sick, or have I turned green or something like that?"

"No, you don't look any different that way," Nanette said. "It's just your expression—like you'd just seen Banquo's ghost or something. What is it?"

"I don't know yet, but it could be something big. Do me a favor and take my pulse. Tell you why afterwards."

"Sure, but—oh!" she snatched her hand back.

"What now?"

"It's nothing. You're cold. It startled me."

"I thought so. Go ahead with the pulse."

She took it, and then stared at him incredulously. Then she took it again.

"This is crazy," she said. "It isn't more than twenty to the minute. Dolph—you *are* sick!"

"No, I don't think so. With a pulse of twenty I ought to be dead. But I feel fine. In fact I feel great. And I think our lives have just been saved. If you watch me, you'll notice I'm not breathing either, except when I talk."

"If you don't stop being mysterious," she said grimly.

"I am going to pick up the nearest blunt instrument and make you good and sick. Talk!"

Grinning, Dolph told her of his experiment with the sap. She was furious; it took him the better part of ten minutes to get her calmed down.

"I know, I know—everything you say is true, but all the same it had to be tried. And look, Nanette: this stuff is better than food. It slows down the metabolism—slows it *way* down about five times. We'll use that much less food, that much less oxygen, that much less water. And there's something else—I'll check this *very* carefully, believe me, but it might even make it possible for us to live outside without masks, at least for a few hours at a time during the day. We'll save on heat, too—I'll bet my body temperature's going to wind up at about half normal—and we'll be glad of that in about a year."

"Why a year?"

"Because then it'll be winter. The Martian seasons are twice as long as they are on Earth."

"Hmm. I still think it was foolhardy, but...I want to try it."

"No," Dolph said firmly.

"Don't give me that. If you can make a nitwit of yourself, I can too. And if there are any benefits, I ought to be entitled to them."

"No argument—but the experiment's less than an hour old. The stuff could still kill me. Even if it doesn't, there may be long-term bad effects—what the doctors call chronic toxicity. And then there's this business of feeling so good; it's like a drug. Maybe the sap's addicting."

"Even if it is, there's obviously plenty," Nanette said, but she did not press the point. "O.K., I'll hold off for a little while, anyhow. How long are you going to insist upon?"

"Oh—say a week. Not really long enough, but it'll have to do. I want to experiment with the dose, too; maybe I took more than I need, or—well, we just don't know yet. What now?"

Nanette had cocked her head, and had stopped listening to him with more than half her mind.

"Listen to the wind. That's not just the evening blow. It's getting worse."

After listening a moment for himself, Dolph had to agree. "I wonder what that means?"

"Didn't you say we had nearly a year to go until winter? Then we're just at the beginning of autumn here. This is such a small planet, the winds must change pattern pretty sharply with the seasons. And I think it's just started to change."

"I think you're right." Dolph strode to the porthole and looked out. "Look at that sand! It's getting thicker every second. This could be a bad one."

Nanette nodded soberly. "If you ask me," she said, "that week is going to be a long one."

9. THE LONG BLAST

Nanette was right. That night's sandstorm was only half an hour longer than usual, but the next morning's was better than an hour longer; and as the week wore on, the situation worsened steadily. By the end of the week, there was only about an hour around noon (and, presumably, another around midnight) when the air was quiet and clear. It was evident that the porthole would be covered shortly—and after that, perhaps the house itself.

Their only hope lay in the fact that the wind continued always to blow in the same direction—though now from the south. Both the change and its constancy baffled Dolph for quite a while, but finally he thought he saw glimmerings of an explanation.

"Look," he said, drawing a circle on a scrap of left-over wall-paper. "I'd be a lot surer of this if we had an outside barometer—come to think of it, it ought to be a snap to build one—but as a theory it makes sense. Say this is Mars, looking down on it at the North pole at the time we arrived—just before the equinox, when the equator is warmer than the poles, just like it is all

year round on Earth. While it's like that, the air ought
to circulate like it does on Earth. Here's the direction
of rotation, counter-clockwise. Now—" he quickly
sketched in something like a ship's propeller, its centers
at the pole, its blades bent away from the direction of
rotation—"that gives us a traveling wave up in the
stratosphere, a jet stream, like this, going in and out
toward the pole twice a day but blowing in the same
direction the planet rotates. Of course that never touches
the ground, but—" he put in four ovals trailing after
the "blades" of the "propeller"—"it trails four high-
pressure spots out toward the equator, and those give
us our dawn and dusk winds. If we were farther north
or south, say at about forty-five degrees of latitude as
we were in Iowa, we'd hit low-pressure cells that would
have the same effect. So that's why the weather always
moves from west to east, just as it does at home."

"Which is why the wind is blowing steadily north
now," she agreed gravely. "Brilliant, Holmes, brilliant."

"No, it isn't, idiot. Now winter is coming on, and
winter on Mars *isn't* like home, because then one Martian pole is warmer than the equator—which never
happens at home." He drew another circle. "Here's Mars
in winter. Then the wind blows from one pole to the
other, going along the ground from the cold pole to the
warm one, and back up and over through the stratosphere. And it'll go right on like that through the sol-
stice to the next equinox."

She considered this in silence for a few moments.

"It makes sense, all right," she said at last. "And I
don't think I like it, Dolph. With the wind blowing from
the cold pole steadily, all the time, for nearly a year—
well, it's going to be cold around here."

"Sure it is," Dolph said. He took her hand, tentatively. "But look, Nanette, we knew that already. We
knew it before we ever left the Earth—we just didn't
know exactly why. Even at noon it won't get above
freezing around here, not by more than ten degrees at
the most, and it'll be blowing all the time. But by being
here, we've got a break we couldn't have expected or
foreseen at home: the tumble-lichen sap. If that works

out, we won't be too awfully cold, and we'll come through."

Nanette closed her eyes, and slowly shook her head.

"What's the matter, Nan?"

"Dolph, Dolph—the lichens will all be buried. They may be buried already. *And they die in winter*—we saw that from the Earth, too!"

After a moment, Dolph put his hand to his forehead.

"That's true," he said, stunned. "That's true... Nan, we've got to go out."

"Into that storm?"

"Yes. We don't have any choice. We can still dig in the lee of the house—the 'shadow' you talked about. We'll have to, before the sand gets any deeper. We have to pack the lean-to full of lichen, while we can still get it. Otherwise, we're dead."

"All right," Nanette said. "Then pass the bottle, Dolph."

"The time isn't up."

"I don't care. I won't go out into that storm without some of that juice under my belt. If I do, neither of us will come back."

There was no arguing this. Silently, Dolph put the wine-press into action. Despite the gloominess of their situation, he was forced to chuckle at the parade of expressions that crossed Nanette's face as the elixir took hold. If he had looked like that when she had first seen him after he had tried it, he could understand why she had been alarmed.

"Wow," she said. "That's great. I don't see how anything that good could be poisonous."

"I just hope that doesn't come under the heading of famous last words," he said. "But we've got no choice— we can't get along without it, now. Better get dressed now—the sand out there's getting deeper by the minute."

They managed to dredge up several bushels of tumble-lichen during a quiet noon, before the storm drove them inside again. This in turn yielded about a pint of sap— enough to last quite a while, for Dolph had discovered that a tot of it barely large enough to swallow was sufficient to carry him through a full twenty-five-hour day, while a larger dose, while it exerted its effects somewhat longer, was in the long run wasteful. Nevertheless, they lost no opportunity to augment the supply, for—as Nanette had reminded him—when the winter had firmly closed in there would be no more lichens to come.

For the rest of the time they were hard put to it to fill up the hours, for though there was much that they needed to be doing to provide against the future, most of it could not be done while the storm raged. Nanette had adopted her own, originally half-frivolous suggestion of keeping a diary. There had been a great deal to record in it at first, but as their confinement wore on the entries became shorter and shorter. Nevertheless, she kept at it, for even a bare notation of the passage of a day had the minimum virtue of keeping their calendar up to date.

"I wish we could have some light, though," Nanette said. "Not to stay up at night with, but for days when the weather is like this. Since the sand started blowing I can hardly see what I'm writing. Can't we spare the electricity, now that the windmill's working? Or is the battery going to go dead on us some day, too?"

"The batteries are new, and this type ought to be good for any number of rechargings," Dolph said. "And we can take power directly from the generator as long as the wind blows. But I'm just not up to making a carbon filament—and besides, even if I could, and got a bulb blown, I couldn't evacuate it...Hmm. Don't need to. I could just take it outside and seal it up out there—200 millibars of nitrogen ought to be nearly as good as a vacuum for this purpose. I'll think about it—maybe it *could* be done."

While he thought, he busied himself cannibalizing the antigravity rig to build a crystal radio. It had occurred to him that it might just barely be possible to pick up one of the strongest of Earth's broadcasting stations, or at least one of the networks if all the stations in a network broadcast on the same frequency—a question to which he could not remember the answer, if indeed he had ever known it. In the loneliness and silence of Mars, even the lobotomized ravings of WABC might occasionally be a welcome reminder of home, however tenuous.

While he worked, the wind blew on monotonously, and the sand mounted toward the bottom of the port-hole. The oasis was an oasis no longer, but a well of red murk, except at noon when the sun shone briefly down upon endless waves of cinnabar dunes, none the less depressing for a wild and patternless beauty, like a sea of blood frozen in mid-tide.

"What are we going to do for light after the sand piles up over the porthole?" Nanette wanted to know.

"Go out and shovel it away, I guess."

"What, Mr. Edison—still no magic electrical glow-lamp?"

"Nope. Just shoveling."

"Pooh. And I always thought space travel would be glamorous."

But at least she still seemed to be cheerful—or was making a brave show of it. Perhaps the elixir helped; heaven knew there was little enough else to be cheerful about.

The storm did not stop at the end of a week, but by the end of two it seemed to have reached a sort of in-flection-point, after which it carried away about as much sand as it brought in; though by then the burden of detritus was high enough to require daily trips outside to clear the porthole. By then the radio was almost finished, and high time, too. The circuit had not given Dolph any trouble, except with his memory, but con-triving an earphone—he would have preferred a loud-speaker, for Nanette's benefit, but he did not have the necessary transformer to drive one—had almost de-feated him. The design was simple enough but he had no piece of steel thin enough to serve as a diaphragm; in the end he had manufactured one out of iron filings embedded in baked tumble-lichen resin. It was not as flexible as he would have liked, but he thought it would serve.

For several evenings thereafter, his cat's-whisker probing of the ether—or whatever was doing duty for the ether these days—brought him in nothing but the faint wash of background white noise which is the sound of stars—the "music of the spheres," plus occasional bursts of aural hash which were most probably static from the Sun itself. Evidently no A.M. signal in the standard broadcast band was powerful enough to push its way through the Kennelly-Heaviside layer of Earth's atmosphere and have enough strength left over to reach Mars. Too bad; he had half expected it, but still it would have been pleasant to have been able to pick up a little music now and then...to say nothing of an occasional human voice, were it only some pitchman touting headache pills. Instead, the only man-made signal that came through the earphone was the steady *flickflickflick* of his own pump, like the distant sound of someone single-mindedly dusting a piece of wire screening with a whisk broom.

The other signal, when he finally found it, was markedly softer, but there was no possibility of its being man-made.

"I don't like it," Nanette whispered, her eyes wide, the clumsy phone pressed to her ear. "It sounds like—like an animal in pain."

"Well, it could be somebody singing—I've heard worse," Dolph said judiciously. "But I don't think it is."

"Then what—"

"Wait a minute, and you'll know everything I know about it. I made up a loop antenna after I happened on this thing. Watch what happens when I rotate it."

Her eyes widened once more. "The sound gets louder!...There, now it's faded again."

"Yes, I swung the loop back out of line. I can't pin it down more than approximately, but it seems to be coming either from west-north-west of where we are—or from exactly the opposite direction, of course. In other words, either from somewhere in Syrtis Major, or in the direction of 'Arabia'. Or from somewhere much farther away, more likely, by the weakness of the signal."

She lowered the earphone and stared at him.

"But, Dolph—that must mean—oh, no! Do you think that somebody's come for us?"

He took the earphone from her and listened for a long moment to that high-pitched, infinitely melan-

choly, ululating whine. It went on and on, as though
the thing that produced it had no need to pause for
breath. The sound went through the inside of his skull
like the pain of a dentist's burr.

"No, I don't think so, Nan. It's far too soon for
that... and whatever else that noise is, it isn't a human
noise. Or any other sound that was ever heard on Earth."

"Then—" She stopped, as though uncertain whether
to be hopeful or alarmed. "Then it has to be Martians!
Oh, Dolph, do you think they might help us? Do you
think they could?"

"I don't see how," he said gently. "They don't even
know we're here—and I'm not so sure but that I'd rather
have it that way, at least until we know more about
them. At the moment we've got nothing to go on but
that noise, and I don't find that any more reassuring
than you do."

He listened to it again, then shook his head.

"As for us finding them—well, at the distance they're
bound to be at, Nan, we couldn't possibly make it without flying. For all the good they can do us right now,
they might just as well be on Pluto—or on Earth, it
comes to just about the same thing in the end."

He put the earphone face down on the table. Nanette
did not bother to nod, but it was clear from her expression that she could not much mourn the evanescence
of a hope so suddenly raised... at the very least, not
this soon.

Outside the house, the long blast blew on regardless.

10. CIRCUIT OF THE SUN

As any student of Dante—or the Arctic—knows, an eternal winter is as close to being an inferno as any living human being is ever likely to imagine—and as Dolph and Nanette found, a six month long winter spent in a primitive hut is not a noticeable improvement. Of course there was never any snow, but fine sand makes a perfectly acceptable substitute, and is even more difficult to keep out of the house. As for cold—mediated though they were by the tumble-lichen elixir, the nighttime temperatures in the house were often ferocious. Outside, they were always so low as to be outright meaningless.

Nanette bore it the less well. Despite all that Dolph could do with jokes, word games, improvised chessmen and sessions of hard physical work—and there was certainly very little of *that* he had to improvise—her innate cheerfulness wilted steadily, melting gradually into becoming morose, sullen and solitary. The small bruises that she inevitably sustained, often simply from bumping into things in the narrow confines of the hut, hung

95

on for weeks, and after a while, too, he began to suspect
that there was something wrong with her eyes.

It was only after two episodes of something suspi-
ciously akin to delirium, however, that he realized that
she was specifically ill. It was most probably a nutri-
tional deficiency of some sort; Dolph had no way to
judge which one, since such things had long been extinct in the part of the world in which he and she had
been brought up, but he suspected beri-beri. Luckily,
it did not seem to be grave, at least not yet; but it
worried him, and even worse, it deprived him of her
help and company alike most of the time.

In her absence, he took on also the chore of keeping
up the diary, and in the remaining time—of which
there was a lot—he listened to the ceaseless, wavering
cry from the crystal radio. There was a pattern in it,
of that he was sure, and sometimes he felt almost on
the verge of grasping it. Then, once more, it would fall
apart into meaninglessness.

He thought that with a cathode-ray oscilloscope and
a high-speed camera he might have cracked the problem in short order—but he might as well have wished
for a million dollars, the Taj Mahal, and a broiled lobster with drawn butter and a spring salad. (Never mind
that.) As matters stood, he had nothing to fall back on
but close listening, patience, and a mathematician's
faith in the existence of order at the heart of every
puzzle, even on Mars.

And slowly, slowly, these began to pay off. His first
assumption, that the noise was in fact a voice—for it
certainly did sound organic, like an animal in pain, as
Nanette had said—he discarded eventually on com-
monsense grounds: nothing animal could go on and on
like that, hour after hour, week after week, not even a
disc jockey who didn't need to breathe. If the message
being sent were both important and unique, it couldn't
possibly be so long—and so limited in range. If, on the
other hand, the message was brief and repetitious, as
seemed more likely, it would surely be assigned to a
machine—unless the imagined Martian had a com-
mercial sponsor, which hardly seemed likely.

A machine then; but if so, what kind of a machine,

and what was it sending? First of all, there was the possibility that it was "sending" only by accident, like the noise made by Dolph's pump, and that the sound carried no information (other than being characteristic of the machine that made it). But this was the only such Mars-born sound that Dolph could pick up. This presupposed either (a) that the Martians didn't know how to shield their electrical machines, and that this one therefore was the only one in this part of the planet; or, (b) that they did know how to shield, and had shielded all their machines but this one. Neither notion was logical enough to be worth any more study for the time being.

O.K.; then the signal was machine-generated and repetitious, but there was a message in it—intentionally. To know that much about it already—no matter with what reservations—had to be counted a solid gain. Nevertheless, it was not much more than a beginning.

What might the message be about? Before Dolph could know that, he had to know how he was supposed to be receiving it. True, he had picked it up as a sound, but that was no guarantee that it was being sent out as one; all he knew about that for sure was that it came to him as radio waves which he *could* translate into sound waves, but which the Martians might translate into something else—or might be able to sense directly, as Dolph could sense light waves directly.

Now there was a thought: Supposing the signal was supposed to be translated first into a picture—that, in other words, it was a television broadcast? At first he rejected the notion out of hand, since he was getting the broadcast on a wave-length rather low in the standard A.M. band, whereas television required high frequency. Later, however, he remembered vaguely that very short waves had not been available when TV had been invented, at the dawn of the century. The primitives had sent stationary pictures by low-frequency A.M., and even by wire—

But if the Martian noise were even so simple a TV transmission as that, to translate it Dolph would need a pierced-spiral scanning disc—which he could make—and a powerful but sensitive amplitude-modulated light

source, which he couldn't. All right, scratch that—and
hope that it's wrong anyhow.

But wait a moment; was he giving up too easily?
Any such noise as he was now hearing would not translate into anything but the simplest of pictures—a cross,
say, or an ellipse—and that certainly would not make
a good test pattern for a useful television set. Its very
simplicity suggested that it had been designed to be
easy to pick up, and easy to identify, and over continental distances at that. Dolph could think of only one
kind of signal that would have to satisfy all three of
those conditions:

A beacon.

And what could be *more* likely, on a planet where
the desert was supreme over vast areas for twelve
months out of twenty-four, and even the vastest land-
marks might be obliterated by a sandstorm in a matter
of days? If fixed bench-marks were needed, they had to
be established where nature could not touch them—
except, briefly, with solar static: in the electromagnetic
spectrum.

What Dolph was listening to, unlikely though the
notion was on a waterless planet, was almost surely a
lighthouse.

What use he was going to make of the discovery was
a question for which he could see no answer at all.

He had no more time to think about it now, in any
event, for somewhere on the far side of the dead of
winter, Nanette began to improve slightly, and thereafter was much more trouble than she had been at her
most ill. Dolph was delighted; every other problem but
this went completely out of his head.

The improvement was small enough, in all conscience, but he fostered it like a wren trying to raise a
cuckoo-chick. At first, she only talked in her sleep, and
allowed herself to be fed without objecting more than
feebly to his interfering with her private nightmares,
even when she discovered him sitting with her after a
blackly howling night. Then, she became wakeful
enough at times to become embarrassed that he had
been doing half the sanitary patrol for her while she

had been unable to do it for herself, and he had a hard time persuading her that he ought to continue to do it for a while to conserve her much dwindled strength. He won that one only by reminding her brutally that she was on Mars, which she had mercifully forgotten at her worst crises. After that she was docile, though depressed.

As her spirits lifted, she began to ask that he tell her stories, a task that baffled him completely; though enormously sensitive to the poetry of mathematics, he had no literary imagination whatsoever. The outcome of the proposal was that *she* told *him* stories. This embarrassed him at first, but the tales she invented— fantastic improvisations about six-legged animals who needed boots to ward off a bad cold, dragons abashed to discover that they had fluffy pink wings, bears who went space-traveling in a rocking-chair (well, what really was so fantastic about that, now?)—were so unpredictable, and she seemed to take such delight in alternately surprising and outraging him, that he concluded they were at least as good for her as anything he might have concocted, with talent or without it.

Glad though he was to see her beginning to recover, however, he was nevertheless at a loss to understand why she was recovering—or what it was she was recovering from. He had done nothing for her that he had not been doing all along, and there had been no other change around them that he had been able to detect. For example, his guess that her problem was a dietary deficiency now had to be ruled out; her diet was exactly what it had been for months.

Equally obviously, she could not have had any sort of systemic infection, for had it been acute she would have recovered—or died—much earlier, whereas if it were chronic she should not be recovering now. Had it been simply the blues—a serious depression of the spirit, a kind of poisonous despair, which had expressed itself in a random collection of physical symptoms. That was possible, of course, but it seemed grossly out of harmony with what he knew of her character and her youth.

He let the problem rest for a month, finding no handle by which he could even begin to grasp it with any

confidence. In the meantime, however, her partial return toward normal human converse—slow though it
was—encouraged him to broach the question with her,
once he felt she was strong enough not to be discouraged
by his puzzlement.

She promptly alarmed him all over again by laugh-
ing.

"I've been thinking about that myself," she said.
"There are parts of it that I noticed long before you,
but I didn't want to bring it up because—well, because
well-brought-up young ladies aren't supposed to discuss
such things with males, not even relatives. But I guess
this isn't exactly an ordinary situation either."

"Listen, are you sure you're feeling all right? It isn't
that important, now that you're mending. We can wait
until—"

"No, Dolph, I really am making sense. The thing is,
this planet doesn't have any moons, or at least the ones
it does have are so small that they might as well not
be there."

"Moons? But, Nanette—"

"Hush and let me finish, will you?" she said firmly.
"On Earth the moon is important to all sorts of things,
not just the tides and the calendar. It has something to
do with the weather, and there are lots of animals—
even ones you'd never guess, like fiddler crabs—that
seem to time some of their behavior by it. Isn't that
right?"

"Yes, it is," he said. Belatedly, he was beginning to
see what she was driving at.

"O.K. It affects people, too. That business about crazy
people getting crazier at certain times of the month—
it was even called 'lunacy'—wasn't just superstition.
And *everybody* knows that us female types run on a
lunar calendar... except that on Mars, it seems, we don't."

"So that's it."

"Well, that's part of it, anyhow, I think," Nanette
said. "I noticed that something was amiss not very long
after I got here, and since then just about nothing has
gone the way it's supposed to. I must have got pretty
toxic, and probably my hormones were all out of balance, too. I'm just going to have to adjust to a new

schedule, that's all—and so is every woman who comes to Mars, I'll bet. I'm just glad it's over this time."

"I hope it is. But how can you be sure? Uh, I mean—what do you think made the difference?"

She smiled. "Why, Dolph, that's easy. Spring is coming."

"Spring?" he said numbly. "Yes, I suppose it is. Not that we'll notice any difference for quite a while yet."

"I've noticed," she reminded him firmly. "And you will too if you listen. You've been so busy worrying about me this past week, you haven't even noticed that the wind has changed."

Startled again, Dolph got up and bounced awkwardly to the porthole. Sure enough. The air was still hazed with ochre dust, but the narrowing fan of land where the drifts had been lower, the lee area they had taken to calling "the back yard," showed long feathers of sand curling off the tops of its dunes, horizontal to the building. Gradually, the yard was being swept clean.

While he stared, there was a soft thump from above, like the sound of a cat jumping off a table. He looked up automatically, and then out of the porthole again as two more thumps hit the crate roof. This time, one of the objects came falling into view and hit the ground before him, still rolling before the wind. It was about the size of his head; once, beyond question, it had been much bigger.

It was a tumble-lichen fallen into the oasis after having been blown across a thousand miles of steppes and clefts. It was not as pretty as a first robin but it was a thousand times more welcome.

Spring was indeed begun; the "wave of quickening" was on its way north from the melting and subliming polar cap.

But no buds showed, and no birds sang; it was still cold as death outside, and the air as thin and lifeless as it had always been, and always would be. Only the gradual replenishing of their food supply, and the still more gradual rise in the noonday temperature maxima, showed that the grip of winter had broken. They were still confined to quarters, except for the briefest of forays to collect lichens and clean the pump-filter. At least these broke the monotony of their days, a little.

Except for the journal, they would never have noticed the day when an Earth year had passed since Dolph's spoiled landing. The Martian year was not much more than half over—how much more, it was hard to guess, for Dolph and Nanette had necessarily been counting Martian days, of which there are 668.6 to a Martian year. By Earth time, the Martian year is 687 days. Either way, however, there were better than 200 days to go to the end of the first Martian year.

To the eye, nevertheless, the oasis outside the crate and the lean-to softened as the days wore by. As the wind lessened, the periods of good visibility began earlier in the morning, and ended later in the afternoon. The lichens spread gradually, too, not just occasional migrants now, but establishing themselves on the floor of the crater. The time was foreseeable when there would be a carpet of them again, as unbroken as it had been when Dolph had first seen it.

The moderating weather suggested to Dolph the possibility of exploring the oasis, at least in short forays in the hours bracketing noon. Though he was reluctant to admit it, what he was hoping to find was an artifact— any object, no matter how small, how old or how broken, which had been made by some guiding hand and brain, not just a product of nature. It seemed to him that by Martian standards, this valley had to be considered so sheltered and verdant a place that it must be known to whatever entities were responsible for the mysterious radio signals. Even if they were not using it now, he reasoned, they must have visited it at some time in the past, and left some sign of their passage, even were it only a few pieces of their equivalent of garbage. There was a lot one could learn, after all, from midden-heaps.

But they found neither midden nor artifact. If the valley had indeed ever been visited, the visits must have been brief and far apart—or too long ago to have left any traces Dolph's inexpert eye might recognize. Of course, Dolph's and Nanette's brief, random diggings hardly qualified as skilled, intensive excavation, but Dolph was reasonably sure that had there ever been a lot of traffic in the oasis, they would have hit upon some sign of it. There was nothing.

They did, however, find something that Dolph thought might be of even greater value to them in the long run: a Martian animal, of a size large enough to suggest that it might be practicable to eat it.

Nanette at first rejected this suggestion with horror, for the creature was not pretty. It was a hard-shelled, reddish invertebrate which combined the best features—or, from Nanette's point of view, the worst—of a centipede and a scorpion. It even had a sting in its tail, suggesting that somewhere on Mars there were animals its own size, or larger, against which it might have to defend itself. It was a burrower, coming out only at dawn—which explained why they hadn't seen it before—to feed on the mites and nematodes, and harvest water from the lichens. It had twenty legs, moved rapidly when the sun warmed it, and seemed to vary from about seven inches in length to nearly two feet.

Nanette's verdict on this complex biological wonder, so beautifully adapted to its world, so recognizably obeying many of the evolutionary laws which prevailed on Earth, yet so obviously neither an Earthly creature nor related to any, was classic in its simplicity: "Ugh."

"Very ugh," Dolph agreed. "But a real find, all the same. I'll bet there's a lot of meat in those claws, and probably more along the sides and back too—it'd need lots of muscle to run all those legs, and make the tail strike as hard as it does." The toe of his shoe carried a respectable slash to testify to the force with which the animal could drive its stinger. He suspected that the sting was venomous, too, but had absolutely no plans to test the theory.

"Dolph Haertel, if you're suggesting that we eat that thing, I'll just leave you flat. Starving to death would be a lot better than—ugh!"

"I'll bet you've eaten lots of things like it."

"I have not," she said indignantly.

"I seem to remember that you love crabmeat—especially from those huge Alaskan king crabs."

"Well—all right, yes, I do. But I don't have to think

about the crab while I eat it. Any more than I have to think about a pig while I'm eating bacon. This thing is different."

"Nanette, put your hand on your heart and swear to me solemnly that you have never, never eaten a broiled lobster straight out of the shell. Now look at our friend here. He could almost *be* a lobster if it weren't for the extra legs. Isn't it true?"

Nanette looked stubborn. "I see what you mean," she said. "I agree that there's a likeness, I admit that the first time I ever saw a lobster I was horrified—I'll admit anything you like. But I will not eat that monster."

"Well, I won't insist," Dolph said with a sigh. "But I mean to try it. One thing that's been worrying me is that our diet is awfully short on protein. This looks like a good source of it, if it's edible at all. And I want to build up a lot of strength for summer. I've got a really major project I have to try—not just simply surviving, but actually trying to make things better."

"What is it?"

"I want to climb up to the rim of the oasis."

"What on—on Mars for?" she said, aghast. "Why, Dolph, that's miles up—and no breathable air at the bottom, let alone at the top! It'd be like trying to climb Everest in your underwear!"

"Not quite as bad as all that. Remember, I weigh much less here than I did at home, but I've still got the same muscles I had then—though I'll have to be in better shape than I am now."

"But *why?*"

"I want to set up some sort of simple radio jammer up there," Dolph said earnestly. "Not to send any message, but something that might scramble or fuzz up that beacon we've been listening to. And loud enough so that the Martians—if that's what we're dealing with here—can pinpoint where it's coming from."

"Great. We louse up their beacon, make them mad, and give them our names and zip code numbers. Then *they* eat *us,* and our troubles are over!"

"It could happen that way. But I'm hoping they'll be more curious than angry. Remember, we don't know a thing about them; we're not even sure they exist. But if they do. I want to attract their attention. I think we have to.

"In fact, I'm sure we have to. Nanette, we've been doing better at getting along on Mars than anybody could have expected. We've got good reason to be proud of ourselves. But it just isn't good enough. One more bout of sickness—or some other accident, something we can't even guess might happen now—and we'd be done for.

"Somewhere up there, there just may be intelligent creatures who could help us, if we asked them to. And I'm going to, Nanette. We need help."

PART THREE

Visitors

11. HIGH GROUND

Designing the jammer took considerable thought. It had to be simple (as did all their improvisations), portable and capable of putting out a lot of noise over a relatively long time. For power, Dolph decided, nothing would be a more suitable source than the wind; it would be erratic, true, but less so than an Earthly wind, and it would last longer than his device; which was more than could be said for any accumulator he might devise with the materials at hand.

He had no hope, of course, of matching the complexities of the Martian signal itself, but any spark that would produce a tearing burst of white noise across most of that band should prove quite annoying enough. for his purposes—if anyone was listening at all, the sole hope behind the whole project.

This time, furthermore, it could not be fragile—not only because he would not be around to service it if it broke down, or replace it if it gave up, but because he had to climb the crater with it. During the course of that climb he could at best expect to knock it several times against one outcropping or another. At worst he

might drop it—but nothing he could build could be
proof against that kind of fall, despite the weak Martian
gravity. His building materials were too closely limited
to such stuffs as coins, glass and old string, whereas
rock was rock, even on Mars.

The final product looked as gimcrack as all of his
other constructions, but it was, bluntly, the best he and
Nanette had been able to do. He thought it would serve.
Essentially it was an anemometer which whirled one
set of unevenly wound coils inside another, passed on
the resulting power to a set of small sparking brushes
which spun on the same shaft, and fed the signal to an
antenna which was one end of a wavelength-long spool
of copper wire, drawn hair-fine, the other end of which
Dolph planned to throw over the cliff once he was at
the top.

This Rube Goldberg device packed into a frame about
the size of a cigar box and weighing less than a pound.
On test, even in the moderate winds of the oasis it
produced in the earphones a weak but strident whistle
which varied in pitch with the wind velocity; Nanette
found the noise almost as unnerving as the beacon whose
operators it was supposed to annoy, and sounding together they produced a wailing the like of which had
probably been heard before only by Dante. When they
crossed they produced most satisfying bursts of white
noise, unpredictably but frequently.

"I'd hate to have to try to screen that out, even with
a lot of equipment on tap," Dolph said. "It's so wobbly
that the only sure way I can think of to deal with it is
to pour on more power and drown it out—and if the
integrity of their signal is important to them, those
white spots will still annoy them over long distances."

"It seems like such a small nuisance," Nanette said.
"Like a mosquito. It's hard to believe they'll notice it."

"The mosquito knocked out the Roman Empire,"
Dolph said, "and if Gibbon had known that, think what
a lot of writing it would have saved him! I hope we don't
do anything *that* drastic. Anyhow, the thing works. Now
all we have to do is to get it up to where they can hear
it buzzing."

"That's what scares *me*. Oh Dolph, take care of yourself!"

"The very best," Dolph said gently. "You too. Starting now, with early-to-bed. You still need more rest than you've been getting, and I'm all packed and ready—I want to go as soon as the morning winds slack off."

"All right," she said. For some reason, she seemed very dispirited, though she was trying hard not to show it.

In the morning, however, just before he donned his mask to leave the house, she stunned him by kissing him good-bye. Up to now they had been very careful about even the tiniest of touches, much though they both had often needed them. Dolph could only touch her shoulder briefly, jam the mask into place, and blunder out—otherwise he would never have been able to leave at all. He thought it could only make everything from now on much harder.

But in fact, he barely noticed the first five-hundred-odd feet of the climb up the crater's rim.

Five hundred feet, however, is only about a tenth of a mile, and a mile was only half the distance Dolph had to climb to reach the dreary tableland of the Martian desert...two miles, measured straight up; the amount of ground he would have to cover to get there might well add more than another.

Nevertheless, it had to be climbed; and it was climbed.

Except to experts in the sport, accounts of mountain climbs suffer from a certain sameness, devolving from the fact that one mountain is really much like another. It is this situation which drives novelists into enriching fictional cimbs with Abominable Snowmen, mantichores, love triangles and other monsters either irrelevant or mythological. Dolph encountered none of these, but his ascent was no duller or less desperate to him on that account; and besides, it was in many ways unique.

Having to travel masked all the way was a grave disadvantage, but there were other aspects of the terrain which, he was surprised to find, worked to his advantage. One of these was that it was not in fact a

mountain that he was climbing, but a hole blasted into
once-level ground by a random astronomical missile.
Hence he was not faced with sheer, plunging walls of
hard granite, but with the rougher, softer limonite,
which offered a surer footing and many more hand-
holds. Like the lunar ringwalls, the slope of the crater
was relatively gentle. Like them, too, it was terraced,
offering natural levels at which to stop for rest and
food—indeed, most of the terraces were quite broad
enough to sleep on without worrying about rolling over
an edge; keeping himself from becoming frozen solid
overnight, which he had expected to be the most serious
of his problems, solved itself when he discovered that
if he lay down just before dusk, he quickly became the
core of a sand-dune inside which the only difficulty was
breathing. And unlike the lunar terraces, these were
weathered, so that their ledges were rounded, and cloven
by many irregular fissures worn by trickling sand.

Also unlike the lunar terraces were the banks of
rubble which connected these to each other: formations
called talus-slopes, produced by the splitting of water-
bearing rocks by alternate melting and freezing—a
process called, poetically, exfoliation. There was not
much water on Mars, but the melting and re-freezing
required for exfoliation happened every day, not just a
few times a year. These long slides or jambles were a
mixed blessing, for although they offered easier grades
than the rock sides of the terraces themselves, they
were also slippery. After being nearly buried by one
after a flailing tumble back to its base, Dolph tackled
them only with ant-like caution, and climbed fissures
or chimneys wherever possible.

Geology—or areology, if that was what he had to
call it here—had another such trap in store for him.
Limonite is not as crumbly as sandstone, but it is not
very cohesive, either. He found this out the hard way
as he was heaving himself up over the rim of a terrace
when an outcropping moved under his hand and turned
into an independent boulder the size of a barrel. Feeling
it move under his grip was a sickening sensation, but
a frantic lunge and scramble brought him safely over
the edge.

Safely? After a moment he was not so sure. Pausing to recover his breath and his nerve, he watched the boulder fall, and was immediately afraid that the danger had only transformed itself into another guise. The big rock fell slowly, but the weakness of Martian gravity had not changed its mass any. When it next struck the side of the crater, it bounced high, and two companions were tumbling in its wake. Though the slowness of the process was almost dreamlike, it did not seem to take very long for it to churn its way into a sizeable avalanche—and below it, seemingly directly in its path, was the shack, looking from this height as small and fragile as two kitchen matchboxes.

Gradually, however, the terraces intercepted more and more of the sliding masses of rock. When the dust finally settled and he could again see the floor of the oasis, the matchboxes were still there, with no motion visible anywhere near them. It was more than possible that Nanette had never even been aware of the danger, unless she had happened to have been looking up after him during the past few minutes, for the slide had not been heavy enough to shake the ground, and in this thin air had been virtually soundless.

In addition, he could see that his climb had taken him at an angle away from a direct line down to the shack, so that even had the avalanche struck the crater floor, it would probably have missed Nanette by several hundred feet. All the same, the near-disaster made him even more cautious of his hand-holds, and his route still more indirect; which had the effect of slowing him down.

And then, incredibly—for it now seemed to him that he would go on climbing forever, as he had always been climbing—he topped one more crumbling ridge, and the high desert stretched out before him, glowing and still in late afternoon sunlight.

Despite its stillness, it seemed to his dazzled eyes to be moving, in some subtle way he could not quite understand. There was no wind, and nowhere even a feather of cloud—only the dunes, long frozen ripples that told of motion past and movement still to come. But by some oddity of the light, the tilted steppes seemed to be burning, as gently and inexorably as though the

very atoms of the ancient sands were decaying into cold
light before his eyes. A tinge of brilliant, almost electric
blue in the light made the unusual rusty color of the
sand seem almost brown, and the puddles of shadow so
like ink-blots as to seem almost liquid, especially those
made sharper and smaller by distance.

He looked up. Except near the sun, the sky was as
usual dark enough to show quite a few stars; but even
at its blackest, the blue tinge was there. The whole sky
looked as though it had been made from a spill of "wash-
able" ink which had paled a little around the sun and
the stars—not a proper heaven at all, but a dome of
stained crystal, pierced here and there to let in celestial
fires which burned not very far beyond it.

Bemused, Dolph remembered at once a famous medieval woodcut of a man who, having reached the horizon of a flat world, had broken through the crystal of
the sky where it touched the ground and now stared in
wonder beyond the sphere of stars at those prime movers—great wheels and other engines—which kept all
the inner, Aristotelian spheres turning against their
backdrop of eternally twinkling flames. Though he knew
that even the artist had not seen the matter so simply—
that, indeed, the woodcut had been intended only to
symbolize what a philosopher might do only in his mind,
but no man ever in his physical person—Dolph felt for
a long moment as though the *primum mobile* might
well lie and turn just beyond this close, utterly unearthly
horizon, which he had only to cross the desert to touch...

And even to hope to touch it would be death. This
was the high desert of Mars, a terrible vision of dry and
eternal winter, in mid-spring as always. No man would
ever cross it except as part of a fully equipped expedition—or, by himself, in a carefully designed vehicle
supported (and, when necessary, succored) by the entire
resources of an elaborate, Mars-based, Earth-supplied
technology. For Dolph, that tempting glass horizon was
as unattainable as Earth itself.

Thus brought back with a thump to the realities, he
set about unpacking his device. But he could not help
wondering about the light. Evidently, this was one of
those rare days of "blue clearing," when the atmosphere

of Mars, usually as opaque to blue light as all atmospheres are, had suddenly become transparent to the shorter wavelengths of the visible spectrum. The effect had often been noticed—even photographed—on Earth.

All very well, except that as an explanation, it didn't explain. Here on the spot, he could no more guess what caused "blue clearing" than could Earth's astronomers. But the effect was certainly striking; in fact, it was downright eerie, like a landscape remembered from a nightmare.

The jammer seemed to have suffered no damage during the climb. Finding a shelter for the machine which would protect it from the sand—without at the same time shielding off a part of its output by the iron-rich rock—was out of the question, and in any case would have defeated the whole purpose of his climb: the anemometer cups had to be out in the open, preferably as high up as possible. He settled eventually upon a sharp rise with a flat, mesa-like top, on which he anchored the device with heavy rocks—not nearly as heavy for their size as he could have wished—upon its base flanges. The cups were already rotating in the rising breeze of evening, and an earphone check showed that the complex signal was being generated as strongly as before.

The last move was to throw the aerial reel over the lip of the crater. Since the floor was already a well of night, he lost track of the spool quickly, and so could not tell whether it had unreeled all the way, or had become arrested on some terrace.

Well, that could be checked easily enough during the climb down, simply by following the aerial wire as a route-marker. But that was for tomorrow morning. Dolph made camp; and for the rest of the evening, watched the Earth set after the Sun behind the glass horizon, until it grew too cold for him to stay outside his pup-tent any longer.

The return was in many respects harder than the climb up—in part because he had now to be looking down much of the way, and in part because the route laid out for him by the aerial wire had been chosen by gravity without regard for such human conveniences as hand-holds. Experience, however, steered him around the worst traps and troubles, so that in the long run he managed to make the journey a little faster than he had made the ascent.

But when he got back to the shack, he found Nanette ill again. Not seriously, no; much of it, obviously, was simply the product of loneliness and suppressed fear, and within hours of his return she was almost her old self again.

Nevertheless, it was clear that he could never again dare to leave the oasis by himself...nor did his memory of the high ground give him any reason to think that they could dream of crossing it, even together. For better or for worse, this was where the line ended.

12. "THEY ARE NOT DEAD!"

In the Arctic lands of Earth, spring is so bitter and summer so short that the ground only a few feet below the surface never thaws. This iron-hard layer is called the permafrost; and it was something much like this relentless stratum that the Haertels and the Fords had long since struck in their attempts to rescue their children.

The trouble lay partly, of course, in the distances involved—and not only in their sheer size, but in the way they fluctuated, which in turn affected the twenty-five-month time lapses between years when a flight to Mars looked even slightly feasible. In an era when spaceflight of a sort had been a fact for more than two decades, the Moon at a quarter of a million miles away seemed to be nearly in Earth's back yard to people who thought about the matter at all, though nobody had set foot on it yet; but Mars—though there were plans, on paper, to go there—still seemed quite a different matter. The forty-eight-million-mile gap between the two planets still looked vast to begin with, and on closer examination it also turned out to be a fiction—it was

117

only a mean distance, not a real one, and the actual
abyss a spaceship would have to span on such a journey
was never going to be less than eight times as far—at
least not as long as "spaceships" meant "rockets"—since
the destination, like the home port, is always in motion
and must be chased.

Nevertheless, those paper plans to go there did exist,
and several unmanned vehicles, beginning with Mariner 4 in 1965, had paid the little planet visits of sorts.
The real barrier was the permafrost that lies beneath
the surface of all large governments, no matter what
name they go by: layer after frozen layer of official
indifference to any project not close to home in some
way, and not likely to pay off—in votes, in prestige, or
simply in color—during the effective lifetime of the
office-holders who might be in a position to do something about it. There was no deliberate cruelty behind
that indifference; only a kind of practicality which was
worse than cruelty in its confessed and deliberate short-
sightedness.

Four bereft taxpayers in Iowa were in no position to
thaw such a glacier. Not that the families' long and
determined campaign had made no impression whatsoever. The case of the Children in the Sky, though it
had been out of the news for more than a year and was
considered closed, had left a lasting memory trace. Indeed, one widely syndicated columnist had even ob-
served its anniversary by demanding to know what the
government was doing—though he knew the answer
well enough, and was asking only in hopes of embar-
rassing the administration, which was his stock in trade.

And the campaign had left them with at least one
official friend: Garth Marshall, the research director of
A. O. LeFebre et Cie., a huge industrial complex which
subcontracted rocket stages, solid propellants and many
more highly secret objects to N.A.S.A. and the Department of Defense. The fact that a LeFebre subsidiary
was building about half the hardware for Project Ares
was probably irrelevant; the additional fact that Dr.
Marshall had once been a suitor of Mrs. Haertel's may
have had more bearing on his support. Whatever the
reason, that support was wholehearted, and neither the

Haertels nor the Fords were in any state of mind to question its motives.

But Dr. Marshall had thus far been unable to budge N.A.S.A. a centimeter.

"It's the same old story," he told a family conference—the latest of dozens, all equally fruitless and becoming steadily gloomier. "We haven't been able to do anything on the Ares components thus far (I'm not supposed to be telling you this, of course) but make refinements here and there. Strictly frills and furbelows. They may add some reliability to the mission eventually, but they don't do a thing toward getting it off the ground."

"It's still the question of timing, then," Mr. Ford said. The Haertels had met him only once before the disaster; he had struck them then as an amiable non-entity. Since then, he had somehow simultaneously become both grayer and more forceful.

"Yes, I'm afraid so," Garth Marshall said grimly. "With the timetable for the Apollo program in the same old shambles, N.A.S.A. is having enough trouble getting continuing funds for a Moon landing. Even just plain talk about any manned expedition to Mars now comes back labeled 'premature.' And the Soviets won't budge without our cooperation—naturally enough, since they'll be asked to provide all of the orbital-assembly phase, which is where the really heavy stuff is called for. They don't want to spend the money if all we've got for them to boost is one glider and a flock of empty nose-cones."

"Premature!" Mr. Haertel said. It might just as well have been a swear-word.

"But what's that got to do with anything?" Mrs. Ford said. "I don't want to go to the Moon, Dr. Marshall. I don't see why anybody would want to go there. We only want to get Nanette back, and Dolph. Why can't they help us?"

Mrs. Haertel, who had followed Dr. Marshall's account all too well, put out her hand to the other woman, who grasped it blindly. There was a painful silence.

"They don't care about the children," Mr. Haertel

said. "It's not their fault that they don't. Not their children."

"No," Dr. Marshall agreed. "And besides... well, if
N.A.S.A. ever believed that the kids were on Mars—
which I'm not entirely sure they did—they don't feel
any pressure to rescue them now. They think that Dolph
and Nanette are dead. I've tried hard to sell Ares as a
rescue mission, and I've failed utterly. It's just too late
for that."

"But they aren't!" Mrs. Haertel cried. "Garth—they
got to Mars before anyone else. Doesn't that count for
something? Isn't it stupid to think that they could do
that, and yet not be able to take care of themselves
when they got there?"

"It might have been a fluke," Dr. Marshall said, very
gently. "Dolph's basic discovery certainly must have
been a major accident. I've got a man in my labs who's
worked out a really colossal infringement of Relativity,
derived just from the bare knowledge that Dolph had
some kind of anti-gravity, and nothing more—not from
any knowledge of what Dolph actually did, because nobody has that. It might well give us a breakthrough to
some kind of ion drive, something that might shorten
a crossing to Mars by nearly three months. But I'm sure
it isn't more than remotely related to Dolph's work.
Everybody in the world is stuck for the most elementary
explanation of that. And... we know that Dolph took
off for Mars too soon, before he'd properly stopped to
think about what a dreadful desert the planet is. Nanette left even more precipitately; she may never have
reached Mars at all. They've already worked one mir-
acle. Two is a lot to hope for—more than I can sell,
anyhow. We have to face up to that."

"Do *you* think that?" Mr. Ford said.

"I..." Dr. Marshall fell silent, and put two fingers
to his brow, as though something ached above his eyes.
At last he said:

"I've studied Mars for many years. My company's
spent millions of dollars trying to work out ways for
human beings to live there—skilled adults, backed up
by lots of highly specialized equipment. How two teen-

agers could last one day on that planet, I do not know. I simply do not know."

"But you'll go on helping us, Garth, won't you?" Mrs. Haertel said steadily.

"Yes, Doris, of course I will. I'm just forced not to be very hopeful, that's all."

Mrs. Ford burst into tears, but almost they seemed to be tears of relief. Dolph's foster-father stood up. He looked unexpectedly tall.

"There's got to be some way," he said. "Garth, I don't care what any of the other problems are. There's bound to be a way around them, if we stick them out. But as far as the children are concerned, of one thing I'm absolutely sure: *They are not dead!*"

Dr. Marshall stood up also. "I'll go now," he said. "And I'll keep trying. If I can sell somebody our ion drive... well, that remains to be seen. LeFebre can be as hard to move as N.A.S.A.—one of the penalties of size. But in the meantime—no, dammit, I quite agree with you. They are not dead. I know it. They can't be, that's all."

His face stormy, he stomped out. The meeting was over. It was still as gloomy as all its predecessors had been; but it was not yet despairing. Not yet. Not quite.

Once back in his office, Dr. Marshall locked the door, interdicted all incoming calls and carefully constructed a bombshell. Probably, he thought, it would do nothing but destroy his job, his security clearance and his career, but he considered that the time was now past for half measures. The bombshell might also, of course, turn out to be a dud—and on the whole, he was sure he would prefer almost any sort of explosion, now.

It looked like this:

CONSOLIDATED WARFARE SERVICE
Division
A. O. LeFebre et Cie.
Geneva Berlin Brazilia London Paris Rome Tel Aviv

Office of the Director
Department of Space Sciences
Bethesda, Md.
To: Research Personnel
Re: Booster Program—
    Prime Mover Section

Your attention is called to the relativity discontinuity recently discovered by Dr. Lloyd McCann of our staff (v. *Nature,* whole no. 5463; LeFebre Tech. Publ. 1094; unpublished memo, ARES D—968).

Briefly and non-mathematically, this discontinuity (which we are calling the McCann Effect for short, over Dr. McCann's objections) implies that gravity is a function of the weaker and still unnamed "fourth force," and as such can vary independently of Lorenz-Fitzgerald mass variation. The pertinent field equations also suggest that gravity has polarity under certain conditions, none of which appear to be duplicatable experimentally.

While the Effect has large implications in cosmology and other theoretical fields, immediate interest attaches to its possibilities as an adjunct to rocket vehicle design.

Suggestions are invited as to ways of applying the Effect to the reaction mass, jet flow or (possibly) payload of a space vessel, either chemical or ionic. As there appears to be no present active N.A.S.A. interest in Project Ares or other trans-lunar operations, the Geneva office will perhaps wish to explore the possibility of technical consultation with British, French, Israeli and Soviet contacts. Needless to say, such explorations should be kept on a strictly scientific basis.

Please post.

GARTH MARSHALL

And that, perhaps, was that: either the beginning of a marvel—or the end of two lives, and possibly three. Time, as usual, would have to tell.

The dark cold sleep of permafrost was also on Dolph's mind, though in a considerably more direct sense. Frustrated in even his hopes of quitting the crater for high ground, he had turned defiantly in the opposite direction: straight down.

He was hoping, in fact, to dig himself and Nanette a water mine.

He was from the beginning almost sure that such a project was feasible, the only important qualification being how deeply he would have to dig before the sands defeated his efforts to hold them back. There was, after all, much more water on Mars than the most optimistic scientific estimates had hazarded—not only enough to cover thousands of square miles of one Martian pole with hoarfrost (or perhaps even snow), but also enough to account for all the water in the bladders of the tumble-lichens; an attempt to calculate how much that added gave him a figure in incredible millions of gallons.

Obviously the source of so much water could not be on the planet's surface. For one thing, sun highlights would flash off it, which would have been visible from Earth, whereas in a solid century of observation since Schiaparelli nobody had ever seen one. For another, any open body of ice in this thin air would sublime—that is, pass directly from the solid state into water vapor, without intermediate melting. Most of it would remain permanently as finely divided ice crystals in the uppermost reaches of the atmosphere, and the rest would join the hoarfrost at one pole or the other in winter.

The conclusion was inescapable: there had to be ice underground, in considerable quantity—perhaps not just a layer of permafrost, but a whole geological stratum, a sort of "aquasphere" hundreds of feet thick.

They found it within a week of digging. It was not much more than fifteen feet beneath the shifting surface of the crater—which now could be called an oasis in all accuracy, for obviously the aquasphere would be totally inaccessible from the high desert without the most elaborate of drilling rigs.

They shored, shielded and roofed the short shaft with the few boards left over from the lean-to project, filling in the gaps with home-made paperboard. The

result was reasonably strong where it had to be, and
kept out enough wind-blown sand to keep the hole
from filling, although its bottom had to be shoveled
regularly. They alternated at that task, and at the
daily chore of cutting and fetching ice-blocks. The
new water supply took a great deal of wear and tear
off the wine-press, which now needed to be used only
for the extraction of the all-important elixir.

They found, too, that the well unexpectedly sim-
plified the job of hunting the scorpion-like creatures
(which tasted absolutely nothing like lobster, but
were not unpleasant to eat, and were inarguably
nutritious); the scuttling beasts took advantage of
the exposed ice layer for their own watering, and
there were always two or three of them half buried
in the sand-cover atop it in the early morning.

But the well proved abruptly to have another attraction that was a good deal less welcome. Nanette
discovered it, and returned one morning without the
ice-cake she had gone for, and with her eyes wide
behind her mask. She did not need to say a word;
she simply beckoned, and that and her expression
were enough. His slowed heart thudding, Dolph followed her out.

The crude trap that they had built for the ugly
arthropods was broken and empty. Around it in the
sheltered sand were half a dozen broad, regular
markings about the size of a pie-tin. Most of them
were blurred, but one was quite clear and sharp.

It was the print of a heavy, five-toed paw.

13. TRACK OF THE CAT

That motionless, frightening, unreadable hieroglyph in the Martian dust brought back into Dolph's mind another sign that he had been trying—more or less successfully—to ignore for months: the function of the sting in the arthropods' tails. Had the thing not had survival value for the animals, in present time, evolution would have selected against it, and no matter how useful it might have been in the past, today it would be gone or at best only vestigial. Progressive loss of structure with loss of function is one of evolution's firmest decrees—as witness the human vermiform appendix.

"So it had to follow," Dolph said gloomily, "that there *was*—there *is* at least one animal on Mars larger than this invertebrate, that either hunts them, or that it hunts. Well, we can see that they don't hunt anything larger than the lichen mites, themselves. And now we know the answer. We should have been making preparations against it long ago."

"What kind of preparations?" Nanette said, peering out the porthole at the deceptively peaceful noon. "I

don't see any trees to make a palisade of, out there—
or any water to run in a moat."

"I don't know," Dolph admitted. "Electrified wire,
maybe, if I hadn't used up most of the available stuff
making that antenna for the jammer."

"I wouldn't put any faith in anything that could be
jumped over," Nanette said. "How big do you think it
is?"

"Bigger than the crustaceans—that's as close as I
can come. If it were Earthly, I might make some guess
by the size of the track, but we've got no reason to think
the same proportional relationships apply here. Also,
it's a desert creature. It might be pretty small and still
have a big foot to walk on sand with. Like the snowshoe
rabbit—going from *its* track, you might think it was
as big as a dog."

"Well, I'm going to think of this one as being about
the size of a small elephant," Nanette said. "That way,
I won't be upset if it turns out to be only as big as,
say, a large rhinoceros. And now that we've settled
that, just what *are* we going to do?"

"Trap it," Dolph said.

"Dolph Haertel, I knew doggone well you were going
to go too far sooner or later! And once you catch it, I
suppose you'll want to keep it in the lean-to!"

"Well, it's in the back yard already," Dolph pointed
out with a wry grin. "And we've fed and watered it, so
it'll probably keep on coming back. There really doesn't
seem to be much left to do but give it a name; how about
'Bertram'? or 'Pywacket'?"

"You're impossible," she said, for at least the fiftieth
time. "All right, I give up. Why do we want to trap it,
O Mighty Hunter?"

"Well, to see what it looks like, for a starter. Though
since we thought to put the mine in sight of the porthole, I suppose all we need to do is keep a lookout early
in the morning—it seems to come around at dawn, if
we can go by today's performance. But I don't just want
to look at the critter. If possible, I want to talk to it."

"Talk to it! But—oh Dolph, do you think it's one of
the Martians? I mean—somehow I hadn't thought—"

"I know what you mean," he said soberly. "I thought

it was just an animal at first, too. After all, people that
can build radio beacons don't go about robbing traps.
Or do they? We just don't know. All we've got to go on,
really, is one fact and one footprint. I don't want a
dangerous animal hanging around here, any more than
you do, but there's no way I know of to make it go away
now—and frankly I don't want it to go away unless
and until I'm dead sure it *isn't* intelligent. Otherwise
I did all that climbing around last month for nothing."

"All right. I can see that, I guess, even if I don't have
to like it. What are you going to use for bait? It doesn't
need to blunder into a trap to catch one of those lobster-
things."

"No, I'm sure not," he agreed. "I thought I'd try something a little more intellectual. If it hunts those crustaceans, maybe it'd like to have some sort of tool to get
through the shells with—a knife, say. Even if it's a
Martian and he has knives and forks of his own, such
a thing would show him that *we're* intelligent."

"The house and the well show that."

"Hmm...that's perfectly true. Well, what would you
suggest? I don't really want to trap him, physically,
anyhow—even trying that might be dangerous. I just
want to attract his attention, and if the house and so
on haven't done that already, what would?"

"Oh, in that case the knife ought to do nicely," Nanette said promptly. "The house and the well are just
here, but the knife would obviously be a present—I
mean, a gift. That's entirely different."

"Well, it can't do any harm to try," Dolph said. "I
hope."

Dolph made the knife from scraps; he had no intention
of giving away any of his imported, machine-made possessions, and he assumed that almost any assemblage
of cut wood and smelted metal—especially the wood—
would look strange on Mars, and perhaps unique. They
put the tool inside the repaired lobster-trap, which was
secured in turn only by a simple latch, and set the whole
lure out on the dusty ice at the bottom of the mine
shaft.

Whether or not the reasoning was sound, the knife

was gone the next morning; and this time the trap, though left open, was unharmed. For his next bait, after some thought about what else might be both Mars-unique and useful the year round in a desert, Dolph put out a nine-foot length of clothesline. That, too, was taken...which was all well and good in its way, but they had yet to see the taker, which after all was the object of the proceedings. In what he decided would be his last attempt, Dolph now put out his canteen, with a chunk of ice rattling in it to show what it was for. That went, too, and on the fourth day he left the trap empty. Then he and Nanette settled at the porthole for a last vigil.

The great dune-cat came to the shack in the first light of day, and knocked on the door of the lean-to. He was carrying the knife, and wearing the canteen slung around his waist by several turns of the rope. He would have been awe-inspiring anywhere, but here, after so many months of isolation, he was fearsome; but these signs left no doubt that he was intelligent—a tool-using creature—and no choice but to confront him.

Dolph got ready. He was frightened almost speechless—but after all, he had invited this confrontation himself. There was no ducking out of it now.

It was the creature's size that was impressive first of all: even in a quasi-sitting position, he stood a good six feet high at the shoulder. His coarse, shaggy fur—which was tawny, mottled in large patches the exact blue-green of the tumble-lichens—inevitably suggested a wild animal, but except for his lynx-like face and mane he really did not look much like a cat. His stance in the resting position was rather like that of a kangaroo, and his arms (or forelegs?) were almost as short in proportion to the rest of him, although a good deal more powerfully muscled. They terminated in true hands: five long, spatulate fingers *and* an opposible thumb. Dolph concluded that he had been resting on his knuckles when he had made the prints in the sand, with the thumb folded inside the fist. Yet he did not look much like a kangaroo either, despite the presence—unnoticed by Dolph until later—of an abdominal pouch; for one thing, he had no tail, and for another, the legs were obviously as well adapted to running as to leaping.

But it was his eyes that, in the long run, made the deepest and most lasting impression. When fully open—for they could be covered inside the lids by nearly transparent shutters, like the nictitating membrane of a lizard or a bird—they were large, still and an incredible dark aquamarine, like the Martian sky at high noon. Meeting their steady gaze was an almost physical shock. Staring into them, Dolph could not help but be sure—despite the fact that the dune-cat was naked, except for the trappings which had come from Dolph himself—that he had indeed at last met an authentic Martian.

Then the cat moved, very quietly and gently. One paw reached out towards Dolph's head, and unfolded its long fingers. The back of the hand was woolly, but the knuckles were bare and calloused. From the knobby tip of the central finger there emerged an inch-long claw, as curved and cruel as a saber.

Dolph stood still and sweated, listening to the thin sound of the wind, and the abrasive whispering of the sand against his mask. He was as cold as he had ever been in his life.

The sharp claw—why did this creature want, let alone need a knife?—touched first one eyepiece of Dolph's mask, and then the other: *tick . . . tick*. Dolph stood fast, although the urge to flinch was almost more than he could bear.

The paw went back to the cat's tawny side, and then the other arm came up—the one bearing the knife. The blade probed for his eyes.

Dolph would have broken and run then, except that he did not dare to move. The great lynx-head bent down over him gravely, as though trying to decide what was the matter with him. Then the knife, in turn, went *tick . . . tick* against the lenses of the goggles. Dolph felt his eyes trying to cross, and two scalding tears ran down on each side of his nose; but he fought to keep himself looking directly up at the cat's sternly savage face. Somehow, he succeeded.

The cat's hand opened. The knife dropped into the sand between them, and the great beast stepped back.

In a voice like a wind blowing over a thirty-two foot organ pipe, it said: *"Mmrreeornndmmannn."*

Dolph tried to answer, but his mouth was completely dry. Helplessly, he raised his own hands and showed them, open, to the intent creature.

Astonishingly, it nodded. "Dmnn," it drummed inside its vast chest. "Dmmnnn."

"Mnn" Dolph growled hesitantly, trying to make his voice as deep as possible. The result sounded absurdly thin to him; but the cat cocked his head, and the flattened, lynx-like ears tipped toward him, tufts quivering gently in the aftermath of the morning sandstorm. Tentatively, Dolph tried it again, and this time managed to make a little more noise.

The cat nodded again—although Dolph realized suddenly that he could not yet guess whether this spuriously familiar signal meant "Yes," "No," or "Look out!" Deciding to be reassured for the time being, however, he turned slightly to beckon to the cabin porthole, behind which Nanette was waiting and watching.

The long colloquy had begun.

The task of communicating with the dune-cat proved difficult indeed. More than once Dolph thought with rueful envy of stories he had read in which the imaginary alien creatures had come pre-equipped with telepathy, or a mechanical translator. This time, unfortunately, the job had to be done the hard way.

At least, there was no shortage of cooperation. The cat left the camp each day before noon, but he was back each morning, just after the dawn sandstorm had ebbed. Early on, he showed a readiness to help with the physical labor—on one occasion supporting the shoring of the mine while Dolph replaced a timber, in a show of brute strength even greater than the considerable that Dolph had suspected was in reserve beneath that smoothly rippling hide. He seemed, too, to understand the simple diagrams Dolph drew in the sand, although how far or how deep this understanding went was difficult to assess.

The real problem, of course, was language. The dune-cat's mouth and sound-producing organs were simply incapable of producing the characteristic noises of the English language; it could shape only a few simple words and syllables, and those imperfectly and with obvious pain. Dolph, on the other hand, lacked both the length of vocal chord and the chest capacity to imitate the deep-throated grunts and growls which were natural to the cat, though he could manage a few of them well enough to make them understood. As a result, the "conversations" evolved gradually into a sort of pidgin, in which isolated cat-growls and English words were stitched together imperfectly—if at all—with gestures.

Any attempt to reduce this dialogue to the printed word could only have suggested that nothing at all was being communicated, and in fact what little information did pass between them was fairly primitive. But certain ideas did gradually become established. The dune-cat could manage "Dolph" quite well, although the "f" sound was rather slushy, and it applied the name indiscriminately to both of them. (Except for size, Dolph reflected, they doubtless looked much alike anyhow in their masks.) "Dmmnnn" seemed to be its name for itself, which Dolph managed as "Dohmn"; if he pronounced the name with a forced, hollow boom, the cat responded at once.

As for their origin, Dolph's experiments with diagrams soon revealed—to his disappointment—that the cat had only the most rudimentary knowledge of astronomy. His attempts to convey that he and Nanette had come from the blue-green star of Earth were met with flat incomprehension. After some weeks, Dohmn seemed to decide, rather dubiously, that they were visitors from Diemos, and Dolph let that pass for the time being. It was at least a step in the right direction.

There were, it appeared, not many dune-cats: more than twelve, which was Dohmn's unit of counting, but not many twelves more than twelve. Beautifully adapted to Mars though the creature seemed to be, Dolph wondered nevertheless whether it was in danger of becoming extinct. It allowed physical inspection of itself with patient indulgence, and Dolph was fascinated to find that the greenish patches on its hide were not part of

its fur, but a lichen with its fungal filaments deeply
embedded in the skin. The vegetable stuff was not an
infestation, but a commensal partner; it drew nourish-
ment from the cat's bloodstream, but it returned oxygen. The arrangement explained how so big an animal
could live in Mars's oxygen-starved air, even given the
benefits of the tumble-lichen ichor, on which the cat
browsed sparingly about once a week. Its staple food
was the crustaceans, which it killed with one surgical
swipe of a paw. It hardly needed the knife, for the paws
proved to be fully equipped with the saber-like claws,
quite like those of an Earthly tiger but more completely
retractable. Nevertheless it learned to use the knife
quickly, and once dissected a crustacean for Dolph with
all the skill of an anatomist, to show him where the
females carried their eggs; these Dohmn in turn stowed
in his pouch, apparently as rations for long trips.

Ordinarily, the cat was migratory, following the
summer up and down the planet. The oasis was one of
its regular stops or feeding stations, and Dohmn was
able to draw a more than passable map showing the
locations of the others. This Dolph copied carefully,
though the session was a disappointment in another
way: it revealed that Dohmn thought Mars was flat.
The map placed considerable emphasis on an immense,
wheel-shaped area which Dolph recognized as the ambiguous territory Earth astronomers had dubbed *Lacus
Solis*—the Lake of the Sun; why this was important to
Dohmn, he could not immediately figure out.

The map session also established that the cat had
not come to the oasis in response to Dolph's radio jamming, and indeed was entirely unaware of it. This did
not prove that confreres of Dohmn's might not or could
not be producing the beacon signal all the same, but
Dolph doubted it. Dohmn seemed ignorant of elementary electricity, let alone radio.

Nevertheless, he pressed this line of questioning as
rapidly as possible. Nanette was of enormous help as
the subjects of the dialogue became more complex. She
imitated the cat's noises even more poorly than Dolph,
since her voice was higher, but she often understood
what Dohmn was getting at long before Dolph did, and

could suggest ways of putting things in the limited common vocabulary available when Dolph despaired of framing a question at all.

The day finally came, however, when they were able to put the problem to Dohmn with partial success. It was accomplished with a sand-diagram of the crater, on the edge of which Nanette drew a mark like a little sun. From this she drew two lines, 180° from each other, in the two directions from which the radio "beacon" might be radiating, and trailing out into dots in the sand. As she marked the dots, Nanette cupped her ears as if listening, and made the questioning sound.

Dohmn's own ears, which he normally carried flattened along the back of his head, stood straight up, and he bounded away from the diagram as if alarmed. When he came back, he quickly scrawled a huge circle around the drawing with his knife—his usual sign that he did not want the picture erased for a while. Then he charged up the side of the crater and vanished, though it was a good hour before his usual departure time.

Dolph and Nanette waited—they could do nothing else—and after about half an hour Dohmn was back. To Dolph's intense irritation, he was carrying the jammer. Dolph could only hope that he could persuade the cat to put it back, for he did not relish the thought of another climb.

But Dohmn was not ready to listen to Dolph yet. Putting the machine down next to the sand-diagram, he made three long bounds away from it. At each stop, he drew a sun; and at the last, his standard diagram of Lacus Solis. Then he returned for the jammer, and carrying it carefully, planted it firmly in the center of his new map.

Now it was Dolph's turn to be excited. He drew a line from his own diagram to Dohmn's; pointed to all three of them, and then up and out of the crater; and at last, he pantomimed marching. The dune-cat made the questioning noise and marked time in place, with a peculiar mincing gait which would have been funny in so huge a creature if its implications had not been so urgent. Dolph nodded. So did the cat.

"Does that mean what I think it means?" Nanette said, almost whispering.

"I sure hope so," Dolph said. "I still can't believe he knows what the jammer is for—but obviously he's seen something like it before, and is telling us where, and how long a trip it is for him: three days."

"And what's more," Nanette said, "he's willing to take us there. Do we dare to try it?"

"I don't see how we'd dare not to," Dolph said. "And with his help, we just might make it, too!"

14. WHEN DREAMERS DIE

Once they had become settled in their own minds that the immense trip needed to be undertaken, Dolph and Nanette felt daily under greater and greater pressure to get it under way. The prospect of something new, of some unknown but possibly drastic change in their circumstances, made their ramshackle camp seem more and more squalid, the whole oasis feel more and more like a trap.

Yet there was an enormous amount of work to be done before they dared to venture up and out on to the high desert. It seemed obvious that they must take with them every scrap of food, every drop of water and elixir, and every rag of clothing and bedding that they could manage—all this, plus the battery, the binoculars, Dolph's signal generator, a tent, all their line, and such minor items as maps and knives. The risk of gutting the camp had to be run, despite the very good possibility that the trip would prove fruitless and they would need to return to the oasis and set up housekeeping as before. Yet it seemed equally obvious that they could not carry all this on their backs, even with Dohmn's help.

The only possible solution, Dolph finally decided, was a sledge, if Dohmn could be persuaded to help pull it. Nanette queried him with several quick sketches and stances, and the dune-cat assented. Then all that remained was to build it, but it was an emotional wrench to get started on the task, since it required demolishing the lean-to for lumber.

When it was finished, the sledge was a toboggan-like platform seven feet long and two feet broad, with a canted prow and side rails. The rails would help in carrying it up the crater wall, as well as providing handgrips for passengers later. Also for better portage, they distributed the supplies and equipment equally throughout its length; they would reload everything on the trailing end when they reached the high desert.

Next came the making of a harness and a horse-collar for Dohmn—the latter to distribute the mass of the sledge evenly across his shoulders without cutting off his wind, on the assumption—which seemed likely—that he had a windpipe in the usual place. The dune-cat tolerated the fitting of these arrangements with what seemed to be good-humored curiosity, and Dolph surveyed the result with some pride.

"Neat, if not gaudy," Nanette agreed.

"Did you know the Romans never thought of that gadget?" Dolph said. "So they never got half the work out of their oxen that they should have. No decent yoke was invented until the Middle Ages."

"Maybe that's why the Romans needed so many slaves."

"That's a thought. I don't remember Gibbon's mentioning that, either. Now, is there anything around here we can make buckles with?"

"I don't think so. I know how to tie a sliding knot, though. And that reminds me. If we could make some kind of a shoulder pack for Dohmn, it would lighten the load on the sledge while we're climbing the crater."

"It wouldn't lighten it for him," Dolph pointed out, "since he'll be helping to hoist the sledge up, too. But he looks like he could take it, and we could give him the pack afterwards—he could probably find plenty of uses for it. Anyhow, it's worth trying."

Despite the constant emotional pressure to be under way, they worked harder on the project than they had worked since their earliest days on Mars. Made a little morose, too, by the prospect of leaving what despite all hazards and discomforts they had come to think of as home, they were both convinced that they were bound to leave something crucial behind, whose absence would be discovered only after it was too late. Hence, despite their day-end exhaustion, they lost considerable sleep trying to decide in advance what that thing would be— since obviously the whole contents of the house could not be loaded on to the sledge.

On the last day, Nanette firmly insisted that they do nothing at all. She invented a particularly preposterous story, about why a mouse named Aelfrida flunked her Ph.D. exam in Landscape Garbaging, specifically to waste the time with. Dolph actually succeeded in falling asleep before the story ended, which was probably just as well, since Nanette didn't have an ending for it.

They started up the side of the crater after the dawn sandstorm. In their hearts, each wondered if they would ever come back; but the question remained unspoken. Behind them, the watery sunlight crawled down the terraces towards the empty and half-demolished house.

With the dune-cat's help, the ascent took only a day, and they were able to launch their small expedition out on to the desert the next morning. Dohmn pulled the sledge; one human being rode, the other walked alongside until he tired, after the example of Arctic expeditions they had seen pictured, long ago and on another world. The sledge glided almost as easily over the fine sand and dust as it might have over snow, and the dune-cat never seemed to tire.

Dolph's projected route proposed that a good three-quarters of the trip be made along the floor of a tributary of the mighty Thoth-Nepenthes Canal, which passed between their own oasis and Arabia, and hence north-east toward Lacus Solis. On the map, the overland distance had looked short enough to make reaching the canal bottom possible by the second day; and

in fact, they were half-way down the western side of
that vast valley—a chasm which made the Grand Can-
yon look like a scratch on a windowpane in comparison—before night caught them.

Despite the higher air-pressure at that distance below "sea" level, the night was bitter beyond all imagining. They would never have survived it without the
added warmth of the dune-cat, who slept sprawled across
the mounds of sand they had buried themselves in, filling virtually all the rest of the tent space. This inno-
vation made Dolph nervous at first—he was reasonably
sure of Dohmn's good will, but after all the creature
was obviously a superb killing machine about which
they really knew very little—but Nanette accepted it
readily and even with some pleasure, as though the
alien monster were some sort of gigantic Teddy Bear.
Whatever the risks, they could hardly have done without him, and got through the night both unfrozen and
uneaten.

The floor of the canal was warm by Martian standards, and a heavy carpet of tumble-lichen made the
going harder for the sledge. This was compensated for
to some extent, however, by the fact that down here
they were once more able to dig for ice when they needed
it. Dohmn took care of that task, in a great fountain of
sand which took him down to the aquasphere in one
furious five-minute flurry.

Paradoxically, the sound of the beacon in the earphones was dimmer in the canal. Dolph could only hope
that some new shielding factor, perhaps a heavy deposit
of iron ore in the canal walls, was responsible. On the
third day, he was worried enough to ask Dohmn if they
were indeed going in the right direction, although the
compass said that they were. The dune-cat said so too,
emphatically. Dolph let it rest at that—and sure enough,
on the other side of an immense bend which they rounded
on the fourth day, the signal abruptly became loud and
clear.

The fifth day saw the end of the stores. Dohmn pulled
them on regardless, and the sledge, now markedly
lighter, almost skimmed over the sedgy valley floor.
Their heads feeling afloat like balloons with hunger,

Dolph and Nanette clung to the straps and tried to believe that the dune-cat, now galloping ahead of them completely out of control, still knew where he was going and why. The sledge rocked and bucked as the cat picked up speed; the moons scooted through the ink-blue sky; the signal became louder; the sand fountained away behind them; the dust and the cold bit through their masks and clothing...

By noon, half delirious with thirst—for Dohmn still would not stop; he seemed truly to be running away with them, his heavy haunches pounding away at the smoking waves of rust with single-minded, almost mechanical ferocity—Dolph and Nanette were clinging to the rails and to each other. Spraying sand from under its tailboard, the sledge tobogganed down into a narrow col. Cliffs beetled above it, steadily shutting out more and more of the sky.

Then, near dusk, the col widened, and they bounced on to the Lake of the Sun.

Dohmn slewed the sledge to a stop and sat down, his vast chest heaving evenly; Dolph could not remember ever having noticed him breathing before. At his feet, the ground fell away toward a broad, almost circular plain, terraced with ringwalls to a floor as flat as the center of a target. The lake itself stretched evenly out to the horizon, lightly dusted with rippled sand which fumed in a steady wind, from under which there shone forth occasionally a dull green gleam of compacted, ridged ice.

Here was a crater to end all craters—as undamaged and regular as Plato on the Moon, yet bigger from side to side than the Moon's Mare Imbrium. The unthinkably massive asteroid that had exploded this enormous well out of the crust of Mars must have hit very recently, as such events go in cosmic time, to produce so perfectly formed a wound and leave behind a genuine lake of open water, stripped from the deep aquasphere to be exposed to the arid air.

Now, at last, the dune-cat allowed them to make camp, and even took elaborate pains to help them. Relieving himself of his yoke, but without bothering to take off his pack, Dohmn promptly went hunting, re-

turning before long with two of the lobster-creatures—
one the largest they had ever seen. A second expedition
took longer, and produced a cake of ice which on Earth
would have weighed a good forty-five pounds; since the
floor of the col was too far above the aquasphere to
permit digging for such a thing, he must have had to
cut and fetch it from the Lake itself. Then he pitched
in to help dig a tent site and drive stakes.

This abrupt return to cooperation, even solicitude,
was welcome enough, but Dolph could not help being
made faintly uneasy by it. It reminded him disquiet-
ingly of a story he had once read, called "The Price of
the Head," in which a castaway finds too late that the
kindness of the natives is due to his position as the
appointed sacrifice to their gods. He left the thought
unvoiced, however; and in his advanced state of physical exhaustion, no thought could have been sufficient
to keep him awake.

In the morning, Dohmn was eager to be moving again,
but this time without the sledge. Dolph and Nanette
were just as pleased to be able to go without having to
undertake another portage. Not that it would have been
difficult, for the terraces here were broad and shallow,
and not much weathered, strongly resembling a colossal staircase. Nevertheless, the dune-cat did not take
the most direct way down, but instead drew them off
along the circle toward the north-east, descending gradually as he went.

By noon they had reached the level of the Lake, and
Dohmn's apparent goal: a pair of intricately carved pillars at least twenty feet high, cut from the stone of the
ringwall. They flanked an open entrance into the cliff,
of equal height and far too regular to be a natural cave.
Dohmn went in promptly, and then, finding that he
was not followed, sat down on the smooth floor and
made an imperative rumbling sound: "Dohwnn...
dohwnn."

"Don't rush us," Dolph said, peering dubiously into
the opening. "All right, so this is where we were going—
but suddenly I'm in no hurry."

"Me, either," Nanette agreed. "It's pitch black in
there, after the sunlight gives out—and it slants down."

"There's a turn just beyond where Dohmn is sitting, too. What do you make of these carvings, Nanette?"

The girl studied the pillars. "Not very much. They're pretty worn. They seem to be written in columns, like Chinese—or like numbers."

"Which doesn't tell us anything, I'm afraid. We can't even guess whether the characters are alphabet-letters or pictographs. But what I meant was, do you think somebody like Dohmn could have made them?"

"N-n-no," Nanette said slowly. "They're too small. I don't see how those big paws of his could have done such delicate work."

"I agree. So now we're up against creature or creatures unknown. Do we take the chance?"

Nanette contemplated the enigmatic tunnel somberly. At last she said: "Well...whether we like it or not, isn't this what we came to see?"

Dolph donned the earphones and listened for a moment. The beacon was louder than it had ever been before.

"I'm afraid it is," he said. "All right, Dohmn. Here we come."

The darkness in the tunnel was absolute after the first turn. They could proceed only by holding on to the straps of the dune-cat's pack. He seemed to be in no doubt about where he was going, however, and pressed ahead as rapidly as they could walk.

The bend continued, modifying itself gradually into a long smooth curve. After a while, Dolph was almost sure that they were going back the way they had come— but on a much lower level, for the downward slant that Nanette had noticed was continuous.

Shortly, the descent became steeper. The floor of the tunnel was still smooth, which was fortunate, for in the blackness the slightest irregularity would have caused a stumble. With nothing to see and no notion of what was ahead of them, the inhuman, steady yowling in the earphones was almost too eerie to bear.

Nor was it possible, deprived of the sun, to guess at the passage of time. Already it seemed as though they had been sinking into the ground for hours. Curiously,

the air around them did not seem to be colder; in fact,
Dolph thought, the temperature had gone up a little.

After another indefinitely long period, he was sure
of it. On a venture, he took off one glove and reached
out—very tentatively—for the nearer wall. He snatched
his fingers back as soon as he encountered it, but the
expected searing flash of frost-bite did not follow. The
wall was far from warm, but he judged that its surface
temperature could not be much below freezing.

He realized suddenly that it had also felt abnormally
smooth, almost silky; and rubbing his fingertips together, was astonished to find that they were wet. Don-
ning the glove hastily, he stamped and listened to the
quality of the sound. It was distinctly changed.

"What is it?" Nanette whispered, tugging at his belt.

"The texture's different, somehow. We're not going
through rock any more."

"What, then?"

"I'm not sure, but I think it's ice. And it's warmer
here."

"Do you think we're under the Lake?"

"That's my guess." He slipped slightly and righted
himself. "That's ice underfoot, sure enough. I wish we
had a light—now'd be our chance to find out how thick
the aquasphere is."

"If we keep on going down like this," Nanette said,
"we'll wind up under it."

"Yes, if the pressure doesn't close the tunnel up first.
There's a warm draft here—wonder if that helps keep
it open?"

Dohmn growled slightly and tugged.

"All right, all right."

Almost immediately, however, the tunnel walls began to retreat; and so—judging by the echoes—did its
roof. While Dolph was still puzzling over what this might
portend, his straining eyes detected a faint glow, seemingly in the very air around them at first, but bright-
ening with each new step until they could see that it
came from above. The first impression was that they
had come out again, under a dim, overcast sky; but that
of course was impossible. It was the roof that was glowing, enormously far above them.

"Oh, Dolph! Look!"

He needed no urging. As they rounded a last bend, the ground sloped away before them, and at their feet there stretched out the dream-like ruins of a silent, entombed city.

Or was it waiting to be born? The air was warm, moist and thick, almost like an Earthly fog—and there was enough oxygen in it to breathe, for metabolisms slowed by the elixir. The city lay bathed in greenish-gray light, cast across it by the over-arching Lake, which concentrated the distant weak sunlight like a lens.

Dolph took off his mask and earphones, and drew a deep, solemn breath. Nanette clung to his hand. The stillness was profound, and made all the more marked by a far-away trilling of running water...a sound so awesome on this dry little planet that it almost suggested some supernatural presence.

The buildings of the city were tall, slender and widely spaced. Cut from some immemorial crystal which showed not the slightest age or wear, the transparent shapes towered like a convocation of thin ghosts—or like so many droplets of topaz, balanced impossibly upon their narrow ends, their long facets unflashing in the even fill of the light.

Dohmn had stopped, standing erect, silent and motionless as a statue. Inside the clear walls of the city, nothing moved; yet it did not seem dead. Here under all the sand and ice of Mars, it spoke silently for a deep-buried stratum of life—and biosphere, a sheltering place for whatever unknown powers had built this principality, and might still rule it...

The dune-cat made a soft sighing sound, and dropping back to all fours, padded away down a wide avenue—or was it a plaza? There was no time to speculate, or to sight-see; now that he was once more in motion, Dohmn went rapidly. It was odd to see how much at home he seemed here, as though the city were only an extension of the silence of the desert. Here, however, the prosaic Earthly pack between his huge shoulders was ugly; it did not belong to this underworld of silent sky-high jewels.

The doorless towers flowed by. Here and there, fu-

gitive glitters and knots of light shone and vanished
behind their clear dark sides, like the essences of machines also cut from crystal and remembered from a
dream.

Dolph lifted one earphone. The sound of the beacon
still went on inside it, insistent and unchanged, but
somehow it did not seem disturbing any more. It reminded him, instead, of some long aria, like that song
the Sirens sang in Homer; the strident overtones which
had sounded so inhuman before were still there, but
now they were all too human—distortions of the pure
melody introduced by the earphones themselves.

The avenue continued to broaden, as though the
crystal towers were drawing aloofly away from the three
little figures who were following that thread of song
into their labyrinth. At the trail's end, the adamant
pavement swooped suddenly away from the level of the
road into a great pool of light, where the lens of Lacus
Solis came to a focus: a marble-white amphitheater,
with a perfect paraboloid floor which reflected the light
back up against the icy sky in an almost solid-looking
column.

"Dohwnn," Dohmn said.

They went down carefully, crossing terraces which
were too large to be steps, too small to be stone benches.
At the very center of the depression there was another
crystal structure, like a box set on end on a stone dais;
it was perhaps fifteen feet high.

Inside it was a throne. Someone or something was
seated on it.

The figure was not easy to see, for the crystal case
seemed to be filled with some dimly sparkling fluid. It
was tall, and not man-like, suggesting rather a serpent
or worm with a cluster of six or eight small arms near
the head end. On the whole, Dolph was just as glad he
could see it no better.

Then it spoke. There was no visible motion of the
figure in the case, but a deep voice rolled slowly through
the amphitheater. Dolph guessed that it was amplified.
It seemed to have no specific source.

"You are the Earthmen," it said in perfect English.
"Our dune rover has done well; *rrlr-ahmn-oh-ohrr*,

Dohmn. Please come closer, so my machines may sense you better."

The two stepped closer hesitantly. "Who are you?" Dolph said.

"I no longer have a name," the voice said. "You might well call me the one who sleeps. I am the last master of the city."

"How do you know who we are?" Dolph said. "And speak our language?"

"Oh, as to language," the sleeper said, "I know all Earthly languages, except for some minor dialects. All your radio broadcasts reach Mars plainly. As for yourselves, I heard your interference pattern, and deduced your presence, as I assume you had planned."

"Yes," Dolph said. "We were hoping somebody would respond."

"Not possible. My signal is only a beacon, and mechanical, intended to guide others of my race to this city. As you can see, we were a burrowing people. But today it serves only as a life-signal, to announce that I am still alive. I have heard no other such for many years, so it is probable that I am the last."

"Did you send Dohmn, then?" Nanette asked.

"No, sir," the sleeper said, revealing with that one word how great an information gap still existed between itself and its visitors. "The dune rovers are free agents, though once they were to us rather as your dogs are to you. They are now the coming race here—provided that you will help them, as one creature of light to another. I so charge you."

"We're not doing too well at helping ourselves," Dolph said.

"That will change. After all, you are only the first of many men. Quarry our cities for whatever is there that you may need. It is your inheritance...I have waited a thousand of my years to bequeath it."

"Then you can't help us now?" Nanette said.

"No. My people are already dead, or deep in dreams from which we shall not awaken any more. But your people are coming—indeed, are nearly above us now."

"What! But how—"

"They are on their way; I have heard them. We give

you our world. Use it well; and love and guide our *dohmnimi*, who deserved the best from us."

"I hope we will," Dolph said, shaken. "But we're sort of a predatory race—"

"Yes, you are young—otherwise you would not have managed to come here. But the *dohmnimi* are wise in their own half-savage way. If you abuse them, they will avoid you. If you seek their friendship, they will give you much. The choice is yours; but you will never wholly possess high and ancient Mars without their good will. They have already offered you that, freely, when you were in most need of it. Will you forget?"

"No," Dolph said. "We won't forget. I promise."

"Then my dream ends here. Go now. Your people are at hand. All praise to That Which Dreams and never ceases; I can sleep now. Goodbye, *dohmn* and men."

The voice ceased—and so, Dolph realized suddenly, did the signal in the earphones. There was a long, terrible silence; and then, a low hoarse sound which Dolph would remember all his life. It was the funeral keening of the dune-cat, mourning the passing of old Mars.

Overhead, the new Mars waited.

15. PROJECT ARES

Something had gone out of the city when they passed back through it. The topaz flanks of the towers were dim and lusterless, and there were no longer any lights behind them. Even the air seemed colder.

On the surface, it was brilliant blue-black night, not far from dawn—had they really been underground that long? But obviously they had. Beyond the stone pillars, the dune-cat paused and looked up at the stars. Then, suddenly, he pointed.

At first, Dolph thought he was indicating the racing spark of Phobos. While he watched it in puzzlement, he realized that Phobos should not be visible from this latitude at this hour—and at the same moment, the spark flared, briefly but brilliantly, like a tiny candle. Behind it, two more flares licked out and died again. Nanette gasped.

"Ships!" Dolph shouted. "Quick, quick—the beacon's stopped—we've got to start our generator!"

They scrambled wildly up the terraces. By the time they reached their camp, the sparks were long vanished over the half-circumscribed horizon. Dolph got his sig-

nal going again with shaking hands—this time not to
attract Martian attention, but Terrestrial.

Then they settled down to wait, wondering if they
had dreamed everything that had happened since they
had left their remote oasis—now almost cosy in memory, with the loss of any hope of help from the dead or
dreaming Sleeper to get them back to it. Even the morning apparently was never going to come.

But after freezing eternity the sun shot up over the
rim of the Lake with its customary abruptness—there
was no real dawn on Mars, only an unceremonious blast
of sunlight in a still-black sky—and the thin wind
whirled the sand in spirals over the outspread ice. Still
disbelieving, they watched the sky until their eyes ached
and watered behind the masks.

Nanette saw the skiff first. It grew from a black dot
low in the sky to a thing like a thin bat, and then rapidly
into a preposterous kite-like contraption with enormous, swept-back vanes which seemed only barely able
to keep its needle-slim fuselage airborne. It came skimming down along the Lake to a seemingly certain crash,
and disappeared in a roaring ball of fire which ploughed
a deepening trench all the way across the ice to the
near ringwall.

When the fire went out, the skiff's sails were stripped
and crumpled behind it like so many wadded newspapers abandoned in its track. Its body, however, was
miraculously intact, though half imbedded in the surface of the Lake.

"Oh, Dolph! How could *anybody* live through that?"

"People are tough," Dolph said, smiling tightly. "Let's
go see them. I think they'll be surprised!"

They descended the terraces again, with Dohmn lop-
ing easily behind. While they went down, the dart cooled
with shrill squeaks of metal against ice, and after a
while a beehive on its top turned around solemnly three
times and fell off with a muted clang.

A man in full space armor struggled out and slid
clumsily down to the Lake, wrestling with a U.N. flag
on a long metal spear which kept trying to trip him;
evidently he had not expected any such buffeting as the
morning wind was giving him. When he was sure of

his footing, he planted the flag in the ice with a stab almost as angry as it was ceremonious.

By the time he looked up again, the two ragged castaways and the mottled, spectacularly dangerous-looking dune-cat were grinning at him from a distance of only five or six yards. He simply froze inside his elaborate armor. Under his bubble helmet, his honest, craggy hero's face was a study in disbelief and chagrin.

Dolph stepped forward and held out his hand, pulling Nanette along with him. The spaceman retreated, one elephantine step, and then stood fast.

Then his public-address box squawked and cleared its throat. "Are you—" he said, "are *you* Miss Ford and Master Haertel?"

Nanette laughed, which seemed to upset him even more, but Dolph said gravely: "Yes, we are. And this is Dohmn, the present Jeddak of Barsoom. Welcome to Mars, Earthman!"

The Earthman made a memorable answering speech. He said: "Ulp."

One of the great ships of the Ares fleet came down the next day in a fury of smoke, sand and steam, in response to a terse call from the skiff, and Dolph and Nanette were taken aboard. The subsequent catechism was an involved one; Dolph could not remember having been asked so many questions since he had taken his College Board exams. Gradually, however, he and Nanette were able to piece together a picture of what had happened on Earth that had finally brought Project Ares here— finally, and yet far sooner than they had ever had any reason to expect.

Some of the story was political or diplomatic, and hence seemed likely to remain permanently unclear; though the Cold War had long been over, the governmental habit of "security" had never been entirely extirpated. That part had something to do with Dolph's invention, and with a complex maneuver by some corporation research director which had pressured N.A.S.A. into trying for Mars far ahead of its cob-webbed schedule. Also involved, it appeared, was some adaptation of Dolph's discovery which had led to a vastly improved

form of ion-drive for spaceships—hence the unprece-
dented maneuverability of the rebuilt *von Braun* and
her two sister ships; but this part of the story was especially unclear, since none of the vague references to
the new drive suggested to Dolph that his anti-gravity
principle was even understood, let alone contributory.

The skiff pilot's astonishment, on the other hand,
proved to be entirely easy to understand. He had been
told to more than half expect to find "the children"
alive, for Dolph's jamming signal *and* the Sleeper's beacon had been heard aboard the *von Braun* while she
was still six months away from planetfall; but though
the two signals had heterodyned into one, so that no
source for the absurdly complicated noise could be plotted on a map of Mars, the expedition's navigator and
commander had gone on assuming that Dolph and Nanette—or whichever of them might still be alive—were
to be sought in the Sinus Sabaeus area for which Dolph's
charts had shown him to have set out. The sudden
transformation of the signal into a simpler one, easily
pinpointed in Lacus Solis half a hemisphere away from
where Dolph and Nanette were supposed to be—and
this almost at the very moment that the three Ares
ships were settling into their parking orbits around
Mars—had baffled everyone, and there had been a sharp
argument over whether or not to risk sacrificing the
one-shot skiff (which had been designed for a long slow
mapping sweep of the planet at a lower altitude than
the three spaceships could maintain, not for a hot landing inside a narrow boundary) to the hope of solving a
mystery which close approach to Mars had made more
mysterious than ever.

But the decision had been made at last, for some
reason which the *von Braun*'s officers would not explain
at all, but which made them snicker in stifled voices
every time they thought of it, like so many children
who knew where the Christmas presents were hidden
and were having a hard time trying to look innocent.
Every time that interesting secret was approached, the
questions veered off into wholly expectable quizzing
about Mars—and about Dohmn, who had evidently
given the skiff's pilot a bad shock.

Finally, Dolph cut off the questioning himself. "Dohmn is all right. He's been a big help, and I'm sorry I made a joke about him to begin with—I should have known it would just confuse everybody. He's a member of the new ruling race here, that's all, and a friend of ours. But look here, Captain—we're glad to see you, of course, but—*what is it you're keeping from us?*"

"Nothing to be alarmed about," the skipper said hastily, but he could not quite stop smiling. "Just one more interview. We want you to talk to the mission's bacteriologist."

"Do you think we're carrying some sort of Martian mold?" Nanette demanded. "Why, we haven't been sick a minute since we got here—not sneezing sick, I mean; just undernourished and things like that."

The commander laughed outright. "No, nothing like that. But it's not up to me to explain. Lieutenant Gulliver, will you take our visitors to the xenology lab?"

When the laboratory bulkhead swung back and Dolph and Nanette stepped through it, the last mystery explained itself. The expedition's bacteriologist was Mrs. Haertel—Dolph's mother.

Nothing the least bit unpredictable was said for quite a while; but after the first flurries of surprise and joy, Dolph found that he was feeling a little strange. His mother looked older than he had expected, and markedly thinner. He was reminded that these years must have brought her an ordeal of her own.

It was Nanette, however, who first put the feeling into words.

"We're very sorry, Mrs. Haertel," she said. "It was stupid and thoughtless of us, shooting off like that and causing so much worry and trouble."

"It doesn't matter now," Mrs. Haertel said. "I knew all along that you were alive, somehow. You *were* a little hasty, but you were far from stupid—otherwise you wouldn't have survived. I suppose the whole thing, bad *and* good, coudln't have happened the way it did if you'd been older. Your various failures of foresight were just what anyone would expect from teenagers—but on the other hand, once you were here, you saw direct,

simple, unorthodox solutions to a lot of your problems
that would have escaped an adult completely, even an
engineer, because his mind would have been too thor-
oughly set in the conventional grooves."

She smiled suddenly. "In fact, you got the fleet to
Mars, between your precipitateness and Dolph's discovery. Nobody your age has made so much history
since the Children's Crusade—and what you did was
a lot more useful! It isn't over yet, either. There's that
business of the elixir, which may be the one thing that
makes true colonization possible; that, and your deal-
ings with the Old Martian, and much more—why, you're
the resident experts on the planet."

"We didn't do much exploring," Dolph said regret-
fully. "We couldn't."

"No matter. You'll probably be spending the rest of
your lives leading expeditions, now that we've got more
equipment here. Unless, of course, you let us sidetrack
you into being colonial governors or some other such
administrative job." Mrs. Haertel paused and looked at
them critically. "Though there's one oversight we'd better repair right away, before the newspapers get hold
of this story. You'd better get Captain Friedman to marry
you, before he's too busy to pin down about it."

Dolph shot a helpless glance at Nanette, but she
only grinned impudently and offered no help. He said:

"Married! Not that I'd mind—I mean, I think it's a
great idea if Nanette—that is, if you don't think that—
I mean, we're not exactly—"

Nanette said, with the barest trace of malice, "I think
he thinks he's too young. Besides, he hasn't asked me
yet. For all he knows, I might be much more interested
in Dohmn."

"Dohmn?"

"The dune-cat," Dolph said, feeling that the conver-
sation was now utterly out of control.

"Oh, nonsense. Dolph, it's a little late in the game
for you to be gun-shy. If you doubt me, I've got a witness.
Look over there."

For some time, Dolph had been marginally aware
that there was someone else in the cabin: a tall man
standing opposite him, behind his mother and well in

the background. Now, for the first time, he looked closely at the silent shape.

He saw a bearded figure, dressed like Nanette and himself in fresh green Space Force fatigues. His expression was hard to read behind all the whiskers, but his gaze was level and probing. Judging by his color and stance, he had spent many years out in hard weather; he looked lean and competent.

"Anybody you know?" Mrs. Haertel said softly.

"I don't—" Dolph started to say, and then stopped, for as he spoke, the stranger spoke too. He said exactly the same words.

He was, in fact, only a reflection in the polished metal of the *von Braun*'s hull. The tall man was Dolph himself. It had been that many years since he had seen a mirror.

Dolph took Nanette's hand and bowed solemnly to the image.

"How do you do, Mr. and Mrs. Haertel," he said solemnly. "And—welcome to Mars."

AFTERWORD—(30 July 1965)

The manuscript of this book left my hands before Mariner IV reached Mars. Now that the photographs obtained by that marvelous machine have been published, it is interesting to see how far they go toward supporting the picture of the Martian terrain I offered in the novel.

The score, I am pleased to see, is fairly high. The notion that Mars might have sustained an intense meteorite bombardment (a speculation first put forward some years ago by the late Ann Arbor astronomer, Dean McLaughlin) is dramatically confirmed by the photos.

No canals appear in the pictures, so there may not have been as much splitting and tilting of the Martian crust as (also following McLaughlin) I allowed for here. On the other hand, there has obviously been more such tilting than previous theories had suggested; one of the last photos shows a ridge in the Southern hemisphere estimated to be 13,000 feet high. Until now, the only range even suspected on Mars was the so-called Mountains of Mitchell, a ridge near the North Pole which— if it exists at all—cannot be half that high.

Obviously, there is more water on Mars than earlier evidence indicated. This is shown by the wide distribution of frost in the pictures. Before Mariner, the only visible frost was at the polar caps. Since the pictures also show that there have probably never been any seas on Mars, the existence of an underground ice-table also now seems more likely.

Finally, the failure of any canals to appear in the photos does not rule them out. Only pictures Nos. 1, 2, 3, 6, and 8 (of 19 good shots) overlap suspected canals, and the first four of these were taken under high noon to early afternoon lighting, when not even very large features cast any shadows. (Even the craters did not begin to show up well until picture No. 7, taken well across the equator and farther towards twilight.) Picture No. 8 does fall diagonally across one of the most prominent of the suspected canals—but it was winter in that hemisphere at the time, when even the darkest canals seldom show. As one of the astronomers on the Mariner project put it, as a canal-hunter the probe took its pictures "in the wrong places, at the wrong season."

In general, the pictures show an even harsher landscape than I described, but the agreement between them and my description is a good deal better than I could reasonably have hoped.

Winner of the HUGO AWARD
JAMES BLISH

WELCOME TO MARS   63347-7/$2.50
When 18-year-old Dolph Haertel discovers the secret of anti-
gravity, he journeys to Mars in his home-made space ship, and
becomes marooned there when his power tubes are destroyed
during his landing. He must quickly discover the secret to survival on the strange planet—or perish.

FALLEN STAR   62463-X/$2.50
An expedition team at the North pole searches for evidence of a
war between Mars and a now-annihilated planet. Their quest
leads to death, the discovery of an alien in their midst, and to
the frightening realization that their own planet's continued
existence is now in jeopardy.

JACK OF EAGLES   61150-3/$2.75
A fast-paced science fiction-ESP novel, first published in the
1950's and now considered a classic, in which an average New
York copywriter suddenly realizes that he has ESP, and is
plunged into a dangerous world of madmen bent on world
domination.

DOCTOR MIRABILIS   60335-7/$2.95
In this classic novel, Blish vividly captures the life of Roger
Bacon, the brilliant and eccentric philosopher whose radical
teachings and heretical scientific theories led to his persecu-
tion at the hands of the 13th century Catholic Church.

BLACK EASTER   59568-0/$2.50
Theron Ware, the black magician and most satanic wizard on
Earth, is told to unleash the demons of Hell, just for one
evening. But when all Hell breaks loose, Earth becomes the
site of the most unimaginable horror...

THE DAY AFTER JUDGMENT   59527-3/$2.50
The powerful sequel to BLACK EASTER, in which the sur-
vivors of World War III awake to find Satan ruling the Earth,
and become caught in the ultimate battle between good and
evil.

CITIES IN FLIGHT 58602-9/$3.50
AT LAST THE FOUR NOVELS IN ONE VOLUME!
A perennial best-seller, CITIES IN FLIGHT is a science fiction classic. In this tetralogy, the author has structured an entire universe in which mankind is no longer bound to the solar system, but has become both conqueror and victim of the stars.

THE STAR DWELLERS 57976-6/$1.95
When a life form as old as the universe is discovered, its tremendous energy could be of great use on Earth, and man is faced, for the first time, with the implications of trusting an alien creature.

MISSION TO THE HEART STARS 57968-5/$1.95
In this sequel to THE STAR DWELLERS, the Angels, a tremendous energy form, have signed a treaty with humans. But their peaceful co-existence is threatened when a civilization at the center of the galaxy tries to make earth a "subject state."

TITANS' DAUGHTER 56929-9/$1.95
Sena, the blond blue-eyed heroine, is a tetrapoid giantess—taller, stronger, longer-lived, than "normal" men and women. For Sena, who was not yet thirty, the whole world was in the throes of an endless springtime of youth that would last more than a century. But would the jealous "normals" let her live?

AND ALL THE STARS A STAGE 61739-0/$2.25
When the sun explodes, all life will end. No one will survive the blow-up; except the men and women who crowd into a few starships and fly away into space while there is still time, to look for a new home in the infinite void, a new planet on which to settle.

VOR 44966-8/$1.95
Lt. Marty Petrucelli, Civil Air Patrol, USAF, was a bright young man with a troubled marriage, average ambition but an uncanny perception. How was he to persuade the experts of an Atomic Age that the monster poisoning the countryside with radiation was easily within their control?

If you like Heinlein, will you love Van Vogt?

A READER'S GUIDE TO SCIENCE FICTION

by Baird Searles, Martin Last, Beth Meacham, and Michael Franklin

Here is a comprehensive and fascinating source book for every reader of science fiction — from the novice to the discerning devotee. Its invaluable guidance includes:

* A comprehensive listing of over 200 past and present authors, with a profile of the author's style, his works, and other suggested writers the reader might enjoy

* An index to Hugo and Nebula Award winners, in the categories of novel, novelette, and short story

* An outstanding basic reading list highlighting the history and various kinds of science fiction

* A concise and entertaining look at the roots of Science Fiction and the literature into which it has evolved today.

"A clear, well-organized introduction."
Washington Post Book World

"A valuable reference work." Starship